6.99

Palo Alto City Library

The individual borrower is responsible for all library material borrowed on his or her card.

Charges as determined by the CITY OF PALO ALTO will be assessed for each overdue item.

Damaged or non-returned property will be billed to the individual borrower by the CITY OF PALO ALTO.

P.O. Box 10250, Palo Alto, CA 94303

OLYMPIA

OLYMPIA

Dennis Bock

BLOOMSBURY

Published by Bloomsbury Publishing, New York and London.
Distributed to the trade by St. Martin's Press

A CIP catalogue record for this book
is available from the Library of Congress

ISBN 1-58234-023-4

First published in Canada 1998 by Doubleday
Published in Great Britain 1998 by Bloomsbury Publishing Plc.

First U.S. Edition 1999
10 9 8 7 6 5 4 3 2 1
Printed in the United States of America by
R.R. Donnelley & Sons Company, Harrisonburg, Virginia

For Andrea, with love,
and for María.
Siempre

Only what is entirely lost demands to be endlessly named: there is a mania to call the lost thing until it returns.

—Günter Grass

Would it help to announce the problem early on? . . . To issue a reminder that death itself dissolves into mystery, and that out of such uncertainty arise great temples and fables of salvation?

—Tim O'Brien,
In the Lake of the Woods

CONTENTS

ACKNOWLEDGEMENTS

My thanks to the Banff Centre for the Arts, the Corporation of Yaddo and the *Fundación Valparaíso* for lodging and companionship during the writing of this book; and the Toronto Arts Council, the Ontario Arts Council and the Canada Council for making it possible to go where the writing wanted to take me.

I am grateful to the editors at the following publications in which portions of this book first appeared: *Canadian Fiction Magazine, Descant, Grain, Queen's Quarterly, Quarry, Coming Attractions 1997* (Oberon Press) and *The 1997 Journey Prize Anthology* (McClelland & Stewart).

This book could not have been written without the excellent advice of many people. My lasting gratitude to Clare Henderson, Victoria Bell, Bob Ward and Cheryl Pearl Sucher.

Gracias a mi hermano, José Ramón, quien me ayudó a descubrir lo que queda al fondo.

OLYMPIA

I

———⚬———

You wouldn't be able to tell the story from the way Leni Riefenstahl cut the film. Miles of sub-plot and innuendo snipped and tied into dark ribbons and forgotten, reels of broken ankles and bored nose-picking, a fallen ice cream cone puddling a Berlin sidewalk. There were thirty-six seconds of Jesse Owens, the great American sprinter, shaking hands with a German yachtsman named Rudolph of no great fame himself, other than the fact that he returns from the dead in an unrelated fiction more than half a century later. At frame 134, the yachtsman begins to lean forward and whisper an unheard invitation to attend a wedding planned for later that year in Bavaria on the regal waters off the shores of the island castle of King Ludwig II at Schloss Herren-Chiemsee. The sprinter, still breathless from changing the course of history, begins to gesture, steps forward as if to embrace the groom-to-be, perhaps to shove or simply move past him, it's hard to tell, when the outtake cuts at frame 709.

THE WEDDING

WE ARE ALL subdued from the night drive home from the lake, where we have been for the last day and a half, sorting out details with the police. I've had my tie in my pocket since the accident. I take it out and lay it on the wood mantel above the fireplace, beside the photograph I haven't seen in years.

Nobody has said anything since we got in the car three hours ago. The crickets are in full force outside, excited by the thin chemical smell of swimming pools and expensive artificial fertilizers. Silently, my mother carries my sister up to her bedroom, careful not to wake her. On the way home, I massaged Ruby's feet while she slept. I knew her new shoes had broken the skin, though she hadn't complained or said anything the whole time. Only the stove light in the kitchen is on. The refrigerator is humming softly, like a dirge. Outside in the back garden my father's watering the sunflowers, though they're already covered in night dew and fast asleep.

From the mantel I take down the photograph of a group of twenty-two girls. It's been hidden for years behind the giant redwood pine cones my aunt Marian brought when she came from California to visit, and the large dusty candles shaped like eagles. In the picture my grandmother sits in the front row cross-legged and smiling, showing off her dimples and good health. This is her seamstress class, 1927, back in the black-and-white days of uniforms and vocational schools. On the back names and ages are written with little slashes through the middle of the sevens, European style. "Seventeen" is scrawled beside Lottie, my grandmother's name.

I examine each face, imagine the course each life has taken since this photograph was made. I want to believe my grandmother's smiling because they've been let out early that day. And because they're excited. I let my imagination slide backwards. Only a few have ever had their photograph taken. The camera still something exotic, in the same class as the zebra, which all of them have seen but never ridden. They've all looked at photographs in magazines, seen wedding photos, fashion prints, pictures of the war.

There are four girls out of the twenty-two who seem to be taking this picture business very seriously. Two sisters, Louise and Greta Schriebmann, who no one likes to associate with because of their suspiciously dark hair. Last year in history class we studied anti-Semitism in Europe, Germany particularly. We watched films of the liberation of Jews from the camps. The sisters are intense and determined, their eyebrows lowered slightly, teeth clenched. They're standing in the back row—only two rows—so you can't see below their waists. Maybe they're holding hands.

Erika is the third girl. The girl with the long pointy nose. I can see the whole length of her body because she's standing at one end of the group, to the photographer's right. She doesn't want to smile in case the principal of the school asks for a copy of the photograph, which he will undoubtedly do. Since 1921 these class photos have been displayed under glass in the lobby of the college. Erika was gravely impressed the first time she saw them and hopes to affect future generations of students in the same way.

The fourth girl looks more sad than stern. This is Silke, my grandmother's childhood friend. On the back of the photograph, drawn beside her name in a youthful flowing hand, there is a heart pierced by an arrow.

———

Eight months earlier, just back from church on a grey autumn morning, my father's parents come for a visit. I'm signing the box of donation envelopes that my Sunday school teacher has given me, feeling resentful that I have to spend my Sunday mornings at church listening to Bible stories and the holier-than-thou attitude of the other kids in my class. I tell my parents about a holy war going on down there in the church basement, divided into rooms by portable walls and decorated with cloth-and-construction-paper Marys and Jesuses, bright and smiling like little elves. But they don't believe me. Everyone is bent on making brownie points with their teacher in the hope that word will filter upwards to the ears of Pastor Roar, who will either make you an altar boy or not. This is the mark of the model young Lutheran. I have not made it yet, nor do I expect to.

My mother's just fixed tea. Dad's wearing his accordion. He plays in a tango band two nights a week. When he has his way, the group experiments with spiced-up German waltzes.

"You know this one, Peter?" he asks, turning to me and smiling. "'*Muss i denn*,'" he says. "We sing it when someone's leaving. It's a farewell song. Even Elvis did it before he went away to the army." He sings me a verse, the accordion somewhere beneath his voice.

———

Now I must leave this place
And you, my sweet, must stay.

Dad also has a trumpet, upright and untouched in the sun-room on its brass-coloured flowering base, glittering in the half-light of this dim Sunday morning.

Ruby leaves her dolls, looks out the window to the Dodge Dart pulling into the driveway. "Oma and Opa are here," she shouts, the only two German words she knows, though she doesn't know that these words are German. My father walks over to the big front window, his fingers silently playing the last notes of this goodbye song, and looks out to his parents coming up the driveway. He's wearing his grey felt hat, the one with the green-grey ostrich feather sticking out the side. He's had it for years, as long as I remember, and sometimes wears it around the house as a joke. He says it makes him feel like a mountain man, a true yodeller, he says, although he's never gone so far as to actually yodel. He goes to the door, opens it, and says loudly in German, "Just in time for the poppy-seed cake." Ruby's out the door by now and down the stairs, hanging on our grandfather's leg.

I move to meet them, not as excited as Ruby or my father, unhappy with Sundays in general, but glad they're here. My grandfather bows to me in a pretend gesture of formality, and

I respond in like manner. Then I walk down the steps and kiss my grandmother on the cheek. In German she says what I always know she's going to say because she says the same thing every time they come to visit: *Mein kleiner olympischer Spieler. My little Olympian.* Then we speak English.

We walk back up the green veranda stairs and into the house, shutting out the cold air behind us. Today they've brought a bushel of apples. McIntosh are better near Kingston, they say, where my grandparents have lived since coming to this country ten years ago. They always bring us food when they visit, a slice of their harvest. Enormous pumpkins, bushels of peaches and plums. They tell us they pick their apples at a friend's orchard. I can imagine them at it, brisk and efficient, shinnying up ladders, oblivious to the threat of gravity. They are both fit and energetic people. They go on hikes and turn over their generous garden twice a year. When my grandmother isn't gardening, she's preserving their harvest. We have jars of strawberry and rhubarb preserve in the basement, clearly labelled in red marker, along with vats of slowly fermenting, burping sauerkraut. When my grandfather isn't planting or picking, he repairs his friends' shoes. His workshop's in the back room where he used to spend twelve hours a day when he was working at it full-time.

He is a cobbler by trade, a word that rings magically when I hear it.

Today they seem more energetic than normal. They have something to tell us. They didn't call ahead like they usually do. They know we sometimes go for a Sunday drive after church. They probably decided to come on the spur of the moment. I'm thinking this as we sit down at the kitchen table and watch my mother cut into one of her famous cakes. On Sundays we eat like the Europeans do: big late lunches with lots of desserts. They tell us what the drive was like, how the weather is in Kingston. They say hello for the friends my parents haven't seen since they lived there briefly, before I was born.

"Irene wishes you'd come for a visit soon," my grandmother says in her curving Silesian accent. "You don't know how she misses you." I've seen pictures of Irene. She's tall with red hair like my mother's, but somehow American-looking. I remember her dressed in a green, tight-fitting sweater, those circles of big fake pearls wrapped around her neck and wrists. They used to waitress together at the Palm Diner when my mother first came to this country. She claims Irene taught her all the English she knows.

Sometimes my father grows reflective when my grandparents

come to visit—an odd thing, I think, because, as far as I can tell, this is not his natural state. There are so many forgotten habits and memories they bring with them, it seems, along with their preserves or a surprise pair of shoes.

"They started tearing down the corner store," my grandmother says. The store with the old open-top freezer that used to fascinate me on weekend visits when I was four years old. She and I used to step inside on hot summer afternoons and hang our arms into the cool air that lay thickly at the bottom of the freezer like invisible mud. But my grandmother usually stays away from sentimental stories of when my sister and I were younger. She prefers to talk about practical things, as my parents mostly do, not dwelling on the past. *The past is passed*, they always say. Aside from my mother, the Bavarian, they are from Silesia, a part of Europe which they refer to as 'Polish-occupied Germany.' An area known for its industrious and hard-working people, it is an equivocal province, half German, half Polish. A part of the world that's been strangled by history. I have no doubts about how my father and grandparents feel about the past.

But today they surprise us all. We've just finished our lunch, giant gherkins wrapped in veal, stabbed with toothpicks to keep from unrolling. My mother's already doing the dishes. She likes to get things out of the way so she won't have to deal with them later. Calmly, my grandfather picks his teeth with one of the toothpicks he's salvaged from the pile left over from the meal. I'm doing the same. He makes little clicking noises as he sucks his tongue off his teeth. My grandmother's been holding their secret all through lunch, savouring it as she would a special dessert.

"Rudolph and I are going to get married again," she bursts out finally. This sets my father to thinking. I can tell by the eyebrows, cocked slightly at the edge of disbelief. *But you're already married, Mom.*

Instead he says, "Why not, I suppose," looking at the floral wallpaper between his mother and father. "You could start planning right away."

"Oh, we have," she says. All this very brightly. "You know how organized your father is."

Click goes my grandfather's tongue off his teeth, smiling.

Next summer, the day of their thirty-fifth anniversary, they want to remarry on water just like they did their first time around, but this time aboard a rented houseboat on Sturgeon Lake instead of somewhere in the south of Germany. My father's reaction is lukewarm because he thinks the inclination will pass, in the same way clackers and streaking did. He knows his parents better than that. They're strong, not needy of sentimental gestures like the giving and taking of flowers, or hand-holding. They're veterans of Olympia. Together they watched Jesse Owens win gold and saw Hitler rise from his seat and leave the stadium without shaking the athlete's hand. A second ceremony would be going backwards, like returning to a place you left long ago to find only ghosts, or nothing at all. Probably he thinks his parents need short-term plans to keep them occupied, to keep up their spirits. To keep the wolf from the door. Maybe this is why they're so busy with the gardening and the hiking. They need something to do. They're old, after all. This will be nothing more than another seed planted and left for the crows and squirrels to dig up. It's the planting that counts, and not the fact that the seed is thirty-five years old.

We drive to Bobcaygeon, the walleye capital of Ontario, on the edge of Sturgeon Lake where my grandparents have decided to hold their second wedding aboard *Sweet Dreams*. Dad says *Sweet Dreams* floats twenty, but there will only be fourteen of us. On the drive up through the Ontario heartland I think of my father's reaction to the news after the *rouladen* lunch eight months ago, the look on his face that said his parents had finally gone crazy. As we drive north on Highway 35, the radio strangely silent, my mother sits beside him in the passenger seat leafing through *Pattern & Design*, a magazine for people who make their own clothes from scratch, something my mother does. She locks herself away in the room she's named "My Room" and dreams up impossible suits and dresses. The only thing I can tell for sure is that her favourite colours are yellow and green. She scans the drawings for ideas—lapels, sashes, colours, pleats—nervous and a bit impatient. She's already snapped at Ruby and me. Instead of our usual game of I Spy we sit unmoving, hoping for the awkwardness to pass.

I know what my father's thinking. He's thinking about the side of his parents he's never seen before, the part of them they've kept hidden from him like a jewellery box in a secret drawer. Their longing to travel in time, backwards, to a time before he was even born. My father is usually the cheerful one. Level-headed and constant is my mother. Perhaps she understands the problem too, but she's not telling. She flips the page, adjusts her green-and-yellow shoulder.

The low-rent office buildings and factories on the outskirts of Toronto gradually disappear. From the grey cement and shimmering asphalt emerge enormous rectangular blocks of farmland. The emptiness is broken by a straight line of trees in the distance. We pass a modest hut of plywood on the side of the road under which an old woman sits, selling vegetables. Ten minutes later a pick-up truck pulled onto the gravel shoulder with a hand-painted sign propped up against a wheel: Freshe Vegetables. The variation in spelling probably someone's idea of pizzazz to attract city people on their way to and from the cottage.

The feeling of industry is here, although the factories are long gone. Now it's the efficient use of soil. Giant house-like combines silently pick and spray in the distance. Inside one I imagine a scientist sitting at a flashing control panel, a baseball cap pulled back on his head. But as we drive farther north, the tree walls on the horizon become smaller and thinner, replaced eventually by brush and stone. More and more granite boulders lying around, in the middle of pastures, on the side of the road. The Canadian Shield begins to shoot upwards through the earth in the form of granite outcrops and scattered rubble. Lakes appear, small and secretive, dotted with islands.

We've left home early. It's still before noon. My father says we should be at the docks and aboard *Sweet Dreams* by two o'clock. We're already dressed for the wedding. Our mother made Ruby and me try everything on last night to make sure there were no last-minute problems. This, our dress rehearsal, was my mother's idea. Everything was perfect because everything was hers. Designed, cut and stitched especially for the occasion. I'm wearing my first real suit, a soft grey, complete with tie. Luckily a summer suit of light cotton, the pants shortened to the knee. It's hot and sticky out. Even the artificial wind through the open windows brings no relief. It feels like I'm wrapped in soggy toilet paper. My mother's told me I'll have to pull up my long black socks when we get there. Until then I can wear them bunched up around my ankles.

Ruby's wearing a pink knee-length dress with a white sash wrapped around the waist. The new dress is carefully rolled up to her hips so she can feel the breeze on her legs better. Her shoes sit beside her feet, shiny and white and stiff. She hasn't said anything, but from where I'm sitting I can see the brown dot on both of her white Achilles tendons where the new shoes have broken the skin. She doesn't want to bug our mother. We both know the tension in the air. For now, better just to sit.

Our parents are dressed the way all adults dress for weddings. They look serious, important, as if they're going to greet the president of a foreign country, or perhaps a returning

Olympic gold medallist. Ruby and I are not used to seeing them like this. Our father never wears a tie, something he says he's thankful for. He says he's most comfortable with a pencil stuck behind his ear and dressed in his shop apron, which he wears when he works on the sailboat in the basement. He started it last fall, a small two-man racer which he hopes to finish by next year. It's taken him longer than he expected because he only has weekends to work on it. The whole house has smelled of fibreglass for six months. This is something I don't mind, but it troubles my mother. She says he builds boats like boys build model airplanes. Sometimes she says this with admiration, as a comment on his eternal youthfulness. Other times I'm not so sure. This could be something else that's bothering him: a weekend away from his sailboat, his strips of fibreglass, his moulds, his protective goggles. The clothes he's wearing smell of bleach and detergent instead of glue.

We arrive at Bobcaygeon and drive slowly through the little town, observing the 15 m.p.h. speed limit. On the sidewalks people are dressed in short sleeves and cut-off jeans or track shorts. The younger ones wear their sneakers without socks, most of them tanned from top to bottom. You can tell who lives in town. They aren't many among the paler, better-dressed tourists. The townies wear baseball caps, the laces of their shoes broken or missing, scornful of the summer fashions we bring from the south. There are people carrying two-fours of beer from the Brewers' Retail to their cars. It's beer-drinking weather. They know to open their trunks before they buy their beer so they won't have to struggle with keys while their hands are full. Slowly we drive past the parking lot, looking into the popped-open trunks like dentists examining a line of gaping mouths. There are a few Michigan and New York State licence plates. I imagine these belong to the people with narrow heads and large sagging bodies, their children dressed in striped shirts and khaki shorts with zipper pockets.

Our father knows where we're going. We've been here before. We drive over the lock with the white-and-red signs on both sides warning us not to fish from this point. Then turn left, corralled by a driftwood fence into the parking lot of the houseboat rental, the marina where we're to meet between green pine forests and the smooth black waters off the tip of the dock. The parking lot crunches under the weight of our slowing tires.

Everyone's already here, including my aunt from California. After the wedding she's coming to stay with us.

She's been with my grandparents in Kingston since she arrived two days ago. She's wearing a modest dress, almost casual, as if her long journey exempts her from the less comfortable wedding costumes forced upon my parents. At her ankles are the braces she's worn on her legs since she was a girl. When she sees us pull into the parking lot, she hobbles over and sticks her head through my mother's open window and gives her a big kiss. Aunt Marian's a painter. We have some of her landscapes displayed on our walls at home. They show a desert of large purple cactuses and looming blue mountains. My father talks about Aunt Marian fondly, but with a sad look on his face, as if there were something about her that he just can't pin down.

Ruby fixes her dress, my socks come up. I help her put her shoes back on. I take some Kleenex from my breast pocket and quickly make temporary pads for the cuts on her feet. We've never seen or heard of most of the guests. They are all large, a bit tense, showing their teeth through festive smiles. Aunt Marian shows surprise at how much I've grown. This makes me feel obvious, adolescent. I'm intimidated by the grey area between childhood and adulthood. I can't remember much of when I was a boy and I can't see myself when I look into the future. I close my eyes and see my parents, sitting old and toothless in rocking chairs. I see colonies in space. I can even see the day when the planet's overrun by insects. But I can't imagine my part in all this.

There are people here whom I'm supposed to remember from the times we visited Kingston. I don't remember any of them. I try to disguise my perplexed look by facing the sun, by turning the question mark on my face into a squint. The woman who taught my mother English at the Palm Diner hugs me like a long-lost son. Those big pearls grinding into my bony chest. She stoops slightly, too tall to embrace me without embarrassing the both of us. She tells my mother I have an angel's complexion. Then my mother leads Ruby and me over to Pastor Hawking, who is pairing his fingers in the middle of the crowd, graciously nodding his head up and down. I've heard the name before. He's been a friend of my parents since they came here fifteen years ago. He looks younger than my father, but not by much. We share hugs and kisses all around. I watch the grey streaks run through the thick black hair of the pastor's wife as she fingers her own set of pearls. Pearls they are, like milky seeds, but not as proud as the looping circles cast around the neck of Irene, the Palm Diner waitress.

There are also three old women my grandmother's age. It

looks like they've come together. Literally, a set. Sisters, maybe. They're standing at the edge of the crowd, dressed as if by the same designer. They have kind faces, pink and luminescent with age, their heavy bodies propped up on spindly legs. It's obvious that the one in the centre is wearing a wig which, under the bright sun, takes on the light blue tinge of new fishing line. There are more people here. Ruby and I are introduced to them all. We forget their names as soon as we hear them.

The dockhands are getting the houseboat ready for launching. My grandfather has told me with some pride that it's the biggest one on Sturgeon Lake. It's been reserved since last winter. We wait politely on the large wooden dock with white poles evenly spaced around its perimeter, from which hang orange life preservers. The rental office is behind us, beside the parking lot, where people sign receipts and day-long insurance policies. There are three other houseboats, secured by heavy ropes. The rest are already out on the water.

Sweet Dreams is mostly white. A small house-like cabin rises from its centre, a yellow-and-white-striped awning stretches from the stern to the back portion of the cabin. It will provide a bit of shade if the sun proves too much for us in our rich costumes. Up front are neatly arranged stacking chairs, forming an aisle that runs up the middle of the deck to a white altar perched at the tip of the bow. Honey bees buzz in dizzy circles, attracted by the bouquets of flowers placed in white porcelain vases. Everyone boards but my grandparents, who haven't arrived yet. They plan to meet us out in the middle of the lake, chauffeured in a polished mahogany cigarboat—I've seen the brochure—with a tiny Ontario Union Jack sticking out its nose.

People are fishing out on the water, not far from where the houseboats are docked. Any serious fisherman knows you fish for walleye at dusk, or better yet after dark and under a full moon. As I watch them cast out their lines, I wonder whether my grandparents had known ahead of time that they were planning on being remarried in the middle of a full-blown walleye tournament, surrounded by professional anglers from all over the continent. Both my father and I knew this because we were here two years ago, just when the tournament began.

In the middle of the lake we are surrounded by boats of various sizes: dinghies, aluminium outboards, canoes, cruisers. We're still waiting for our grandparents to arrive. The shoreline is clearly visible from here, a clean continuous wall of pines broken only for a moment by a cabin or dock. We're milling about, waiting for things to get started. Everything is in place. All we have to do is sit down. The pastor is ready. After the ceremony we're staying on the houseboat for the reception. The food and drink are set up at the stern under the awning. There is also a squared-off area, possibly a dance floor. Who is going to dance?

Pulling up in a separate boat, where did they get that idea from? Just like their first wedding somewhere in Germany long before I was born. These are all rituals of the land, clumsily transferred to the sea. Limo to the floating church. The only difference is water slows movement, makes things lighter, more dream-like. Probably this is why our floating church is named *Sweet Dreams*.

Somebody's head turns and we all look towards a dock on the far side of the lake. My grandparents. One of the employees from the boat rental helps my grandmother into the boat first. When she gets both feet in safely she motions to the young man. He leans towards her and she kisses him on the cheek. As she does, I see an earring catch the sun like a hot pinpoint. Then he helps my grandfather get in. The pastor's head is still gently bobbing up and down, his smile eager and calm. A few minutes later they pull up alongside the houseboat and are taken aboard. After more kisses and handshakes, my grandparents meet one another at the tip of the bow, nervous as two virgins. The polished mahogany cigarboat with the Ontario Union Jack has returned to the dock at the far end of the lake. Sitting beside the boat, smoking a cigarette, is her pilot, the young man my grandmother kissed, his feet hanging over the edge of the dock, his head turned towards us.

My father has helped everyone to their seat. We are respectful and quiet, as if at a funeral. Silence drops over us and I listen to the lake noises come from all directions, the hum of motorboats, splashing, weak conversations that pass over the flat water like tired sparrows. A speedboat roars by in the distance. The pastor formally welcomes us and thanks the Lord for this beautiful day. I am sitting beside Ruby. Although we know this is a serious matter, we feel like laughing and jumping into the water.

"Dearly beloved," he says. "We are gathered here this afternoon to reaffirm the holy bond of matrimony between this man and this woman." The pastor's head nods more deeply now. He is like a plastic bird poised on the edge of a drinking glass, insatiable, monotonous. On the upswing he looks into the eyes of my grandparents. As he does this the houseboat begins to rock, slowly, once, twice, echoes of the speedboat that has passed by in the distance. Then the big wave comes. The boat jerks slightly, suddenly, and the three standing figures adjust their footing. I am looking at the inside of my eyelids the moment my grandmother disappears over the side. Bright red with white dots following the quick jump and curve of my eyeballs. Voices scream with the rush of bodies to the bow to look over the railing. Like a stone. Down, down my grandmother goes, fading into layers of darkness and shadow and finally and forever into memory.

We spend the rest of the day until nightfall looking for her, some of the men diving in again and again. They slide into the water and return in frantic lunges for air. Those who are young and strong enough. Suit jackets and dress shoes are scattered over the deck. In their shoes, the divers have placed their watches and rings for safekeeping. Those who are too young or too old stand silently and look on in disbelief. I notice with shameful pride that my father stays under the longest. I wonder what he sees in that black underwater forest.

My mother collects Ruby in her arms when the harbour patrol begins shuttling guests back to the marina. She goes easily, drained now and weak from the crying. My grandfather sits in a folding chair, waiting, as if for a train. Alone now, as I've never seen him before. The young man my grandmother kissed is still sitting on the dock, dangling his feet in the water. I can see he knows what happened. It isn't long before the whole lake knows. The authorities begin dragging the bottom in a matter of hours. It's twilight when my father surfaces for the last time and is pulled from the water, panting and blue, teeth chattering. By now most of the guests have been taken ashore. At the stern, early-evening bees gorge themselves on chicken salad and melon.

My parents decide it's better to stay in Bobcaygeon tonight instead of driving all the way home, even though we're unprepared. Between us there is not one toothbrush. Aunt Marian has already taken my grandfather back to Kingston.

We check into a motel with a yellow vacancy sign shaped like a boomerang, its centre directed upwards to the heavens. The motel is just on the edge of town, where the wind in the trees and the thin traffic through the dark drowns out the sound of crickets and bullfrogs. The last available room has only two beds, side by side. I lie beside my sister's small warm body, our parents an arm's length away, and listen to their slow, deep breathing. Crisp foreign sheets prevent sleep. It's years since I've slept in the same room with my mother, in the same bed as my sister. Another move backward in time.

My father's teeth begin to chatter. I hear my mother's hand searching the dark to comfort him, her palm softly cover his crying mouth.

In my dream a silent fraternity of boats gathers in the area where the accident took place, a congregation of those who believe the scent of a drowning attracts prize fish. They risk the chance of pulling her up for the equal chance of bringing in a trophy. I go down to the dock where my grandmother kissed the young man and watch the procession of fishermen float guiltily into the twilight. They don't anchor. They consider the currents and follow my grandmother's slow drift. I know their luck is good, for I hear them pulling the big ones out and the weight of the fish hitting against the bottom of the boats.

At seven the next morning, the motel keeper comes to our door, rubbing his red puffy face. The sun is shining through the spotted window. We're waiting for someone to tell us what to do next. On the brown dresser between the two beds little boxes of cornflakes and a carton of orange juice sit, a still life of this abruptly re-arranged morning. The man at the door tells my father there's someone on the phone in the office. They leave together. While my mother and Ruby wash up in the bathroom, I slip out and walk down to the docks, fifteen minutes along the highway. At the edge of the water I overhear a rumour that someone found an old lady last night on the east shore, tangled in the bulrushes. They say her hair was still neatly tied back, her jewellery shiny in the moonlight.

A weak light from the street lamp opposite the house enters through the big front window. The house is settling into itself for the night. It creaks as the heat of the day drains from its dusty rafters, its secret corners. I'm standing at the fireplace mantel. I remember this photograph from years ago, when I used to play in the attic during the day. It's faded since then, but my grandmother is wearing the same smile, as if she sees something waiting for her on the horizon, something in the future.

There are the two sisters, Louise and Greta, just as I remember them, looking into the camera, uncomfortable. Now I know why they're sneering, half defiant, half terrified. Out of view their hands search for one another, convinced of something terrible to come. And here is Erika, the skinny girl with the pointy nose, efficient and wary. Then Silke, the girl with the heart and arrow drawn beside her name in my grandmother's youthful flowing hand. She hasn't changed either, though so many other things have since this photograph was taken, back when the world was new and alive with light, before there was any need to look back and remember.

II

A man filmed the three boys playing football on Mohrenstraße. Silke sat on a nearby doorstep, knitting. She smiled at the man with the camera. Two Brownshirts came around the corner then. One of the men picked up the ball and kneeled and motioned to one of the boys with a finger. Silke put down her knitting needles and wool and watched her son walk towards the man holding the ball. An old woman sat in the shadows of her living room and looked out a ground-floor window and watched the man with the ball place his right hand on the boy's shoulder and say something to the boy that she could not hear. The man's partner laughed when he made a scissors with his fingers and viciously snipped at the air. Both men laughed when the little boy put his hands between his legs and grimaced. Tears welled in the little boy's eyes. Just then a roar came across the city from the direction of the Maifeld, where the national team had just scored against Czechoslovakia. The photographer propped the camera back up on his shoulder and began to make his way out of the ghetto and back to the stadium.

OLYMPIA

IN AUGUST 1972, just before my fourteenth birthday, almost a year to the day after my grandmother drowned, my uncle Günter came to us from Germany and found cracks at the bottom of our swimming pool. Because war stories had always been a part of my family, I thought I knew something of my mother's brother. All the grown-ups around me then had lived through war, including my father, and everybody had a story they seemed willing to share—friends of my parents, the teller from Frankfurt who worked at the Bank of Montreal at Lakeshore and Charles and spoke to my father in whispers over folded fives and twenties. It seemed that everyone my parents knew back then had escaped to this country from that dark place, as they had, after the war ended. But it took me until that summer to find out that there were things I hadn't been told, that there were secrets in my house.

I knew that my mother spent her war years in the north of Germany, trapped there among falling bombs. She told me about brushing her teeth with salt, the constant drought under her tongue, how they ate nothing but salted cabbage. She told me about the dead man who fell from the sky and lay in the front yard of their house through the month of May and into June and how an old woman from the neighbourhood came by with a bucket of salt every week and sprinkled it over the body to keep the fumes down until the town came and took him away.

She, my uncle, and their mother—the father already half-dead in the salt mines near Odessa, the mineral of dehydration sucking the liquids through his skin, his eyeballs, bringing his lungs, his hunger to the ridge of his teeth. The three of them, six months in a basement. And when the end of the war finally came they were collected onto railcars and rolled over the great smouldering landscape to the shores of the Gulf of Riga where they were released like sickly cattle into a February blizzard. Then hopping trains to get back, holding her little brother's hand dry with fear as they ran, and she the hand of her mother, the three of them grasping for the invisible hand that reached from the tousled boards of departing freight cars and missing, always missing that train, that hand, walking and waiting and running again. Four months to return home and nothing left but stories of salt and drought, stories that in my boyhood meant as much to me as television, as the map of the untravelled world.

Before Uncle Günter came that summer, I found purpose in the meaning of those stories. Even then I used them to protect myself. I needed those train stories to protect me from the other meaning of *cattle car*. But the salt connection didn't occur to me until I saw Günter down there at the bottom of our bone-dry swimming pool. I didn't understand the salt then, what the drought behind my mother's tongue meant, what it was doing behind her brother's eyes. All I saw was the train they rode up to the hanging lip of Sweden. In school we'd seen films of Jews rolling into the camps on those cattle cars, thousands of them at a time. The image of my mother and her little brother aboard one of those wagons shining in my head as brightly as they shot out from those dark spinning reels at the back of the classroom melded with stories of displacement and organized death. After history class I dreamt my mother came to me with forgiveness, sometimes begging. "Peter," she said. "Sweetheart, we all suffered. No one person more than the next." But in my dreams and in my waking life

I didn't believe her. I'd seen those films of men and women and children, ghosts already, waiting to die. I told my mother's story to my teachers and to anyone who would listen. I used it to show how we had paid. That the war had come to us as well.

She was losing water. The summer drought had already been declared. It was in early August, when my uncle and Monika came to Oakville to spend those weeks with us, that we realized where the problem lay. Hairline cracks, practically invisible, were spreading like transparent veins along the walls and the bottom.

Uncle Günter and his wife Monika were from Fürstenfeldbruck, a small town outside of Munich. In the letters we got before they arrived they said they planned to stay with us for six weeks, with a weekend trip here and there around the province and down into New York. They wanted to get away from Munich before the Olympic Games quadrupled the size of their town. But once Uncle Günter saw the condition our pool was in, he wanted to crawl down to the bottom and begin repairing those invisible cracks, a job, he assured my parents, that would take three, maybe four days. That's how he came to take hold of our summer the way he did, and to prolong our thirst.

Günter and Monika spoke German with my parents, although when Ruby and I were around—which was most of the time—Monika spoke English to us in a British accent. She sounded like Diana Rigg from "The Avengers." She had spent the war years in England, she told us. Günter's English wasn't as good as my parents'. I'd long since been unable to hear their accent, but during open house at school and around the neighbourhood I knew it revealed them as the immigrants they were, the tellers of war stories.

Everything I saw in Günter, everything he did that summer, everything I heard him say—in German and in his broken English—I attributed to the war. The war had shaped him like it had not shaped, could never shape, my mother. He was tall, taller than my father, with a sunken chest that looked as though it were pushing the life out of his heart and lungs. At school we called kids like him *fish eyes*. He didn't look at you so much as stare, blinking nervously over those protruding, round mirrors. He was a construction worker, his large calloused hands constantly moving at his sides like the sands of a shifting desert floor.

When we arrived home after picking them up at the airport, we walked them around the house, showed them the guest room with the view to the street and a thin slice of

Lake Ontario, her winding shoreline already receding for the dry air that had been haunting our summer. We took them into the backyard where my mother showed them her garden. Ruby and I followed behind at a safe distance, listening to their foreign voices and punching each other in the arm. My mother pulled aside the browning rhubarb leaves she'd been trying to keep alive beside the peach tree and offered up a scent of hard Ontario soil to her brother's nose. I watched him sniff a stream of dust. His fish eyes rolled back into his head. It looked like he was going to hurt himself. He inhaled a second time, even deeper. *This* was my mother's brother? I thought. My uncle? I watched his eyes roll back around to the world, to me, and a smile pull at his mouth and cheeks. The dirt drained off between my mother's fingers. Ruby gave me a shot in the shoulder and took off around the house.

The five of us walked across the grass and looked down into the dry pit of our swimming pool. My father was the Mister Fix-It of the family. That spring he'd repaired all the eaves on our house in one day. He considered, his hand on his chin. "*Ich habe keine Zeit für solche blöden Sachen,*" he said, pointing over the dry hole and looking at his sister. He didn't have time for such imbecilic things, he said.

Uncle Günter jumped down onto the blue cement of the

shallow end, sank to his knees, and ran his hands over the walls and floor. He closed his eyes. He looked like a blind man looking for a fallen key. He slid on his haunches down into the deep end and did the same thing. When he finally climbed back up onto the deck and started talking in German, I heard my mother and father begin to say no again and again. *Nein, nein, nein.* But Günter shook his head and smiled and rubbed his dry hands together. Monika stood beside me, frowning, but why I couldn't tell.

Günter was bent on fixing our pool. My parents didn't like the idea. He'd flown here with his wife to visit his only sister and the brother-in-law he'd never met before, and their two children, and the first thing he wanted to do was to get to work plastering the walls and bottom of a dried-out hole in the ground. That's not why he'd come, they reminded him. But when they found him down there the next morning slowly sanding the chlorine film and dried algae off the walls, they couldn't coax him out.

"Okay," my mother said in English later that morning on the deck, looking down, a cup of coffee in her hand. "A day or two of this, then the vacation starts." Günter looked up and smiled and gave her a mock salute.

"Maybe this is his way of getting over culture shock," my

father said on the front porch the second night after Uncle Günter and Monika had gone to bed. I was upstairs in my mother's sewing room, my head pushed out into the night. "It'll pass. He'll snap out of it soon."

The great unknown in Munich was who would take home the most medals. How many consecutive backflips Olga Korbut could manage before she spun off into the clouds. The sound of my uncle working in the backyard drifted through the open living-room window while Ruby and I, dressed in matching tracksuits, watched the Games. We were both going to be Olympic gymnasts. Ruby lay on the floor, her chin cupped in both hands, studying the impossible postures of her heroes. She sat in the splits for hours at a time. I did one hundred push-ups every morning and held handstands during commercials. The Canadian team was twelfth out of fifteen. I fantasized about how things would be different if I'd been born Romanian or Russian or Japanese. Anything but who I was.

Around our house that summer the great mystery was how long Günter could sit at the bottom of our pool drinking cups of coffee and saying *"Verflixt heiss!"* to himself as he dragged his plaster-covered sleeve across his forehead. Every afternoon when my father got home from work he found Günter in the kitchen leaning against the counter drinking coffee, the peach or gooseberry or rhubarb pie my mother had made for that evening's dessert sitting half-eaten on the table. In the next room Ruby and I dreamed of gold medals and of our first real swim of the summer. Rain threatened but never finally came. It hadn't rained since early July. It felt like the whole town was burning up. And at five-thirty I watched a frown fall over my father's face as he walked past us on his way to the bathroom to get cleaned up before supper.

I felt the tension seep through the wall of that foreign language that first Saturday with my uncle and Monika. It was a hot and sticky evening. We ate at the picnic table under the tall pines in the backyard. I felt something when my mother and Günter spoke to each other as clearly as a hand brushing over my face. But something as subtle and indistinct as water draining from the shell of our pool. I imagined she was upset because her brother was denying something of her hospitality.

"Beautiful," my father said, sensing something dangerous. I bit into my hamburger. "One of the biggest jobs we've ever done." He began to tell us about the boat he was designing at the shop, a sixty-footer on order from Bermuda. Then, for Günter's sake, he switched into German. I wondered if the

Bermudan team had won any medals so far. Monika was sitting across from me. I put down my burger, reached for the wine bottle beside her plate, and filled her glass. My mother was always reminding us to be polite. Monika pulled her long hair behind her ear, touched my arm to say enough. Her touch ran to the pit of my stomach like a vein of butterflies. My uncle looked at me from the other end of the table. I blushed. My father stopped. Neighbours on the other side of the cedar fence were playing croquet. Someone gave the ball a good whack.

"We got a bronze in sailing today," I said, clearing my throat. "Soling class." Monika looked at me blankly, then shook her head. "That's a three-man keelboat. You guys got a bronze in the Flying Dutchman class." I looked at Günter when I said "You guys," and blushed again. Monika had a beautiful face. There was a silence. She looked at me and pulled her hair back behind her right ear again. Women my mother's age never wore their hair below the shoulder. My uncle sipped his wine. My mother looked at me and smiled.

"Looks like we're neck 'n' neck," my father said, coming back out to English. "A bronze each."

I think my father was the first one to see how things were going to go between my mother and uncle from that time on.

When the silence came the following evening, he quickly asked Ruby and me to put on our own little Olympiad. Right there, in the middle of dinner. "Okay," Ruby said happily, without any coaxing, and bounced across the parched grass before our mother could protest, cartwheeling and backflipping and spinning through the air. When she came to a stop, panting and smiling, she threw her arms up to the sky and thrust out her small chest. My father stood up in his seat. "The judge in blue awards a perfect ten." When she came back to the table, I jumped up onto my hands, the world turning upside down, the grass suddenly my sky, and held the earth against my palms and fingers as long as I could. Atlas inverted. From there I saw my uncle staring at me stone-faced.

Ruby scored higher than I did, but I knew that was because she was younger and that our mini-Olympics were meant to bring us together. I knew they were meant to head off something coming between my mother and my uncle. And for a while they did. That evening after supper Monika sat in a lawn chair out on the grass with her wineglass hanging low to the ground, whistling out scores along with my parents until the August light began to fold in upon itself and the sounds of croquet balls and the splashing of distant swimming pools grew faint and cool around the neighbourhood. When

I let go of the earth for the last time that evening and returned to my feet, blood resuming its equilibrium, my uncle was gone.

We began clearing away the table, everyone except Uncle Günter taking his or her share back to the kitchen. He was standing out on the front porch, alone, his hands in his pockets. I saw him there when I delivered my first load of dishes. Back out by the picnic table, I saw my father walk across the lawn and pause at the edge of the dry swimming pool and look down at the hard, cracking cement. I watched his face drain of all the joy that had filled him at our performance, all the pleasure that had been his, as if that empty hole in the ground were sucking up his vitality and his pride. No one else seemed to notice his grief the first night he stood at the edge of the pool, shaking his head in disbelief. At the time I didn't think it had anything to do with Uncle Günter's slow work, or the tension between my mother and her brother. I thought it was my grandmother. How she'd drowned the year before. I guessed he was looking for her down there in some way. These people had brought from Germany unwanted memories, unwelcome stories, along with their appetite for wine and reparations. I guessed he was thinking about losing his mom.

By late August, Olga Korbut was wowing the whole world and Uncle Günter was up to eight coffee breaks a day. He wanted to stay down there. Working and standing around. My mother and father wanted him out. Monika had taken to borrowing the Chrysler and disappearing every day. I guessed she'd had enough of waiting for Günter. She drove to the Elora Gorge, Niagara Falls, Buffalo, and Detroit. She went to Toronto a couple of times a week, to London, to Kingston, and Wolfe Island. When she was gone, when an event Ruby and I didn't much care for came on TV, we went out to the backyard, hung our feet over the side, and watched our uncle stand around at the bottom of the pool. On the grass we played under the sprinkler to bring home to him our desperation, our need of water. I thought the pool would remain dry forever. I walked around the house all day, drinking water from a glass. Günter had become a fixture down there, his trowel, the cement mixer my father had reluctantly borrowed from a friend from work, the three moon-eyed bubbles of the level watching his slow dance among the forgotten artifacts at the bottom of a dried sea.

One day, after playing in the sprinkler, we sat on the deck with our glasses of water and listened to Günter speak to us. Neither of us understood a word. For the whole afternoon he told us what sounded like stories. We sat there, embarrassed to stop him, forced to listen to the end of his ramblings, sipping, forever sipping. Sometimes as he spoke he became angry and then immediately fell silent, or laughed and slapped an open palm against his thigh. We sat at the edge of the hole in the ground and watched him move like a lion in a pit among his tools, picking up things and examining them, holding them up to the sun as he spoke. Clouds of dry cement dust rose from below and slowly enveloped us and caked our throats. He covered palm-sized patches of wall as if throwing a white cloth over an old movie set from *20,000 Leagues under the Sea*.

On a Saturday after supper, after Günter and Monika had been with us for three weeks, my parents left me in charge of Ruby. They took Günter into the city to go dancing at Club Edelweiss, a German-Canadian restaurant where my father sometimes played accordion with a band, or soloed for small parties. When my uncle reluctantly agreed to go, Monika suddenly developed a headache. She said she was tired from her day of sightseeing. She sat on the front porch with Ruby, a glass of wine in her hand, and waved when the car pulled out of the driveway. I went around the back and climbed into the pool for the first time.

I crawled around in the shallow end like Günter had that first day, exploring. I kept my eyes open. I didn't know what to expect. But I wanted to go deep. I wanted to find out something about my mother's brother. I knew nothing but the war stories, the outstretched hands reaching for freight trains. In *Decisive Decades*, our school history text, I'd read about the Potsdam Conference, the great shifting of borders after the Control Council agreed to deport more than six million Germans beyond the Oder-Neisse line. I knew this was the uprooting of my mother's people. But about Günter himself I saw now that I knew very little. On my haunches I slid down the dusty incline to the deep end and felt the sides of the pool squeeze the world into a box of evening sky above my head. At my feet extension cords twisted like snakes, trowels sharp and weapon-like, a sawhorse, the three-foot level, a half-used bag of cement, and an old red toolbox.

"You don't want to be anything like him, do you?"

I looked up. The sun was settling behind the apartments across the street from the house. A last shaft of light spiralled between the buildings and lit up Monika's face at a ninety-degree angle, collecting in the glass in her right hand. "What's down there for you?" she said.

"I dropped something."

"Well, get it quick and get back up here or he'll rub off on you," she said. Then she walked away.

In the kitchen the next day, while I was getting a handful of cookies for Ruby and myself, Günter came in and said in his broken English, "I need help. Come here." I didn't answer him. He poured himself a glass of lemonade, drank it down, and walked out of the kitchen. I followed him into the backyard, jumped down into the shallow end, and felt the cookies in my pocket snap into little bits.

"You a smart boy?"

I nodded. "But I'm not very good with my hands."

"Hold this." He handed me a trowel. "Make so." He started smoothing plaster along the north wall of the deep end. I watched him for a minute. He started whistling. Then he stopped and turned to me. "*Ja?*"

I stooped over, took some plaster onto my trowel and stepped up to the nearest wall. I remembered what Monika had said about him rubbing off on me. But he was my mother's brother. What harm? *How would you want him to treat the both of you in his country?* my mother had asked us in the car on the way to the airport to pick them up.

"You watch too much TV," he said.

I was spreading the plaster in broad arcs. I stopped and turned around. "The Olympics are important," I said. "It's the Family of Nations."

"Okay," he said, "get lost."

On a Saturday into the fourth week of the visit—during which not an ounce of rain had fallen from the sky—my mother told us that she'd had enough. We were going to Kelso, she said. We were going to find water. We were going to bathe in clean cool water.

The artificial lake is the main attraction at the Kelso Conservation Area. There are two beaches on the south shore, divided by a grassy hill on top of which sits a parking lot and, on the opposite slope, the outfitters where my father and I had, on a couple of occasions, rented a sailboat. No matter how hard the sun comes down on you there, no matter which shore you stand on, you can always hear the traffic going by on the 401 just beyond the poplar and spruce trees on the north hill. There are rainbow in the lake, too, but I'd never caught anything other than rock bass and sunfish, though I'd always wanted to catch a trout. That Saturday I brought my fishing rod along with me, just in case.

After we got organized in the parking lot, unloaded the

picnic baskets and towels and umbrella and magazines and my fishing rod, the six of us walked down the wooden stairs to the beach like three distinct couples. Monika, her large floppy sunhat flapping like a bird, walked a step ahead of her husband. He looked sullen. He hadn't spoken in the car the whole way up. My mother seemed nervous. She swung the picnic basket about grandly from hand to hand, distracting attention from something. I thought maybe she was thinking about her brother. Then I wondered if it was the memory of last summer that was bothering her, if she was worried about my father. If this trip to water would trigger the memory of his mother's drowning. But my father joked with Ruby and me as we walked down the wooden stairs. On the way here he'd worn a pair of black sunglasses. Ruby said he looked like a gangster. Halfway down the stairs he turned around to us, his rolled-up towel hidden clumsily under his baggy summer shirt like a bag of money, and said in a terrible Italian accent, "Meester Capone wantsa you to doa littlea favore fora la Familia," and Ruby laughed and jumped up for his glasses like a little barking dog. I carried the rod and tackle and the second lunch basket. We'd all changed into our bathing suits at home.

We found an empty stretch of sand at the far end of the first beach, close to an old man and woman. Someone's grandparents, I imagined. But they were alone. No kids. No grandchildren. Their loose skin covered their bodies like a translucent wrap. My father and I smoothed out the hot sand with our bare feet. We laid out our towels side by side, six in a row like the stained-glass windows of a church. We peeled off our street clothes, settled down, and waited to get hot enough to go in. I sat down beside Monika. Ruby went down to the water and waded in up to her knees to check the temperature.

Monika's legs stretched out beside me. She was wearing a bikini. Her long brown hair shone in the sun. My mother always wore a one-piece. No mothers on the beach wore bikinis. No other women had long hair. Monika had never had a baby. Her stomach was flat and her legs were still slender. She was twirling a lock of hair between two fingers, eyes closed. Her right knee was raised slightly in the air, her breasts pulling apart from the centre of her chest in a way that made me want to keep looking.

"Have you caught fish in here?" she said without opening her eyes.

"Some," I said. I saw my uncle watching me over the rim of his sunglasses. I turned away and faced the lake.

There were a lot of people swimming, splashing around on

inflatable mattresses and dinghies. I got up and walked alone along the edge of the water but I couldn't get Monika out of my head. I wondered if Günter had seen what I was thinking. I watched the red and green sailboats out on the lake, their white hulls pulled up on the wind, shining against the water. They picked up speed and skimmed across the small lake, lowered because of the drought, and then, trapped, tacked back against the wind. I tried thinking about sailing, about the fishing I would do later that afternoon, about gymnastics. I tried to think about the Olympics. But Monika kept coming back to me. I entered the shade of the woods and leaned my back against an elm and looked for Monika's pink skin in the crowd in the distance. I waited under an overhanging branch hoping, impossibly, that she'd come to me. I hoped she'd leave my uncle and join me. I put my hand down the front of my bathing suit and conjured the sight of Monika in the lawn chair, her long legs crossed like I thought only movie stars crossed their legs, the glass of wine hanging low to the ground before she raised it to her red lips. I closed my eyes and saw her on the beach in her bikini, her breasts pulling away from her, one towards me, the other off on its own, its hard dark eye staring down a lucky admirer. I cleaned my hands on the grass at the base of the elm, then moved out from the shade of the trees. The warmth of the sun spread over my back. In the distance I saw my aunt take my sister by the hand and lead her over the sand to the water. They both bellyflopped once they were up to their thighs, still holding hands, and came up a moment later in a white froth. I was still trembling. My underarms were drenched. Everybody was in the water except my uncle and me. My father called when he saw me and waved for me to come in. Uncle Günter sat watching all alone up on the beach, his sunglasses pulled up over his face. I wondered if he knew what I'd just done.

After lunch I took my fishing rod and tackle to the other end of the lake and fished the small stream that fed the reservoir. From there I could see the two beaches stretching out over the opposite shoreline, the hill rising between them like a broad nose. With my hands I dug up some worms, put them in the small plastic container I kept in my tackle box, and slid the first worm along a size-fourteen hook. I threw it out into a pool and let the worm sink to the bottom. I caught a trout for the first time in my life. Slick and spotted, he was beautiful. I killed him with my penknife and dropped him into a plastic bag. He wasn't a prize, but he was big enough to keep. In an hour I caught three more pan-size rainbows. Before leaving the stream I rinsed the blood off the fish. I carried the plastic bag in my left hand as I walked back to the beach. It thumped against my thigh with every step. By the time I got back a little puddle of blood had formed in the heavier corner of the bag.

When I held it up for everyone to see, Ruby made silly noises and plugged her nose. My mother peered down over the lip of stretched plastic. I told my father what I'd used, what part of the stream I'd fished, how each fish had hit. With a finger under the gill, I scooped up the biggest trout and held him in the air. Monika leaned on an elbow. I described how I'd moved each one to the top of the pool and enticed them to jump by lifting the tip of the rod against the sky. The old couple listened to my story from the next set of beach towels. My mother emptied out what was left in the cooler, a bit more egg salad and some juice, and laid out the trout side by side. I looked at the grandparents again after she closed the lid. The man was rubbing lotion onto his wife's shoulders. I watched how he warmed the cream in his large hands before spreading it over her skin. She faced the water. Her head moving gently with his rubbing motion. That's when I saw the numbers tattooed like dark crawling ants into the loose white skin of his forearm.

My mother sat in the shade of the umbrella. She was flipping through a magazine with Ruby, the one she always had lying around, *Pattern & Design*, pointing out the dresses and sweaters she wanted to make for her for the fall. Monika was still in the sun. She was working on the last of the wine from lunch. After the fish went into the icebox she'd stretched out on her back. There was a line of sweat in the slight crease of her abdomen.

"The wind's good, Peter," my father said. "What do you say?"

I grabbed my shirt and we started for the stairwell. But my heart sank when I heard Günter's rushed footsteps coming up behind us in the parking lot. I wanted my father to say that there wouldn't be enough room in the sailboat, which wouldn't have been stretching the truth that much. But I knew he wouldn't. Maybe he thought Uncle Günter was coming around. Maybe he was coming out of the brooding that had possessed him since he arrived because they were leaving soon. Maybe he was making it up to us.

My father put down the deposit and left his driver's licence with the man at the desk. We got number 45, a blue two-man Laser. Although I knew there'd be no problem with three people, I wanted the man at the desk to say that one of us would have to sit it out. New regulations on crowding. Even if it was me. But he only nodded his head and smiled. He helped my uncle and my father lift the boat off the racks. They carried it over the gravel driveway and nosed it into the lake. I followed behind with the life jackets and tossed them into the cockpit.

"Let's see if we can break the sound barrier today," my father said once we got started. We began slowly, cutting through the water, tacking our way out of the shallow bay. There were other boats in the middle of the lake, small, no other blue ones except ours, different colours cutting across the water like coloured shark fins. As we made our way to tap into the stream of wind that swept across the middle of the lake, I noticed that Günter wasn't comfortable out here. In the sailboat or on the water, I couldn't tell. But I knew right off that he didn't know anything about sailing. He hadn't come swimming with the rest of us, either. But he followed my father's instructions without questioning—where to sit, how to move with the boat. He tried to show interest by asking after the boat's mechanics, pointing to the jib and boom and knocking his knuckles against the top of the centre-board. I wondered why he was out with us.

Once we got to the middle of the lake I saw he needed to sit quietly for a moment and get his bearings. My father was at the tiller, the mainsheet in his left hand. I was at the bow. I knew how to sail, but it was my father's passion and I never insisted on taking over the reins. Anything to do with water my father loved and I wondered at how terrible it was that it should kill his mother the way it had. He'd offered me the tiller a couple of times before we got out to open water, but I was happy to sit up at the bow and watch him work the boat. He was relaxed and smiling, talking loudly against the wind. He'd told me stories about winning this and that cup when he was young and sailed competitively for big prizes on lakes with wonderful names like Ammersee and Königsee, the mysterious mountain lakes of Bavaria, close to Austria and Italy. He'd told me stories of the great yachtsmen he'd met at the Rome Olympics, where he'd finished fifth in the Dragon class.

He pulled us in as close to shore as we could get without crossing the buoys that marked off the swimmers' area to make a pass by Monika, Ruby, and my mother. We waved when they saw us, and Ruby stood and jumped up and down and cupped her hands around her mouth and yelled something I couldn't make out. Monika hoisted her glass above her head and held it there like the Statue of Liberty. We jumped over some small water as we veered full and by out to the middle of the lake. I dragged my hand under the waves, watching my fingers turn pale yellow and then dark like a fish. My hair blew around my face. I looked over my shoulder and saw Günter was smiling now. I heard the ghost of their voices in the wind. The hard German consonants snapping back and forth between them. The gold-medal count, the empty pool, my uncle and Monika—it was all forgotten now with the feeling of water spraying up against my face. I waved to another Laser skipping by off our port side. A red-and-yellow sun stitched into its sail. The air was hot, even with the wind on us and the misting spray coming up off the bow.

As we approached the end of the lake where I'd caught my fish, I pointed to the cove to show my father and he suddenly, unexpectedly tacked to starboard and I went over the side. I didn't have my life preserver on. I saw the yellow-black rocks come up quick against me. I was about to call out, "Trout heaven, full steam ahead!" but my mouth was spreading with lake water and I was sinking. The thought of my grandmother washed over my eyes. Pulled under by the weight of her wedding dress, she must have seen the same things I was seeing now, I thought. The weeds and rocks, a lone fish startled by this underwater intrusion. But before I had time to sink deeper a large scaly hand descended from above and grabbed me by my right arm and pulled me back into air. I breathed. It pulled me up and laid me across the side of the boat. The sail dropped. I started hacking up skunky water from my lungs and spitting up over the edge of the boat. I turned and saw my uncle looking over me, his entire upper body black with water, his hair dripping. My father was still holding fast the tiller, though we were barely moving now. His face was white and stiff with the same look of terror he'd worn the day his mother disappeared into Sturgeon Lake. Saved by my uncle, I thought. The plasterer.

I was okay by the time we got back to the beach. I'd sunk. I'd swallowed some water. That was it. My father had come close to seeing his son follow in the watery path of his mother. But Günter had saved my life. On the way home I leaned forward in the back seat of the car with my hand resting on my father's shoulder the whole way. He'd told my mother, but downplayed the accident. She knew I'd fallen in. I told her I'd had my life jacket on. I owed Günter one. China hadn't won a single medal so far. But in their culture, I knew my life was his now.

Over the next two days Ruby and I circled the pool as our uncle worked, so expectant that we forgot about the Games entirely. He finished the job two days before my birthday, three days before they were to catch their plane back to Munich. The blue paint he'd finished with needed twenty-four hours to dry. I counted on the clock to the exact minute I could turn on the hose, desperate for water in my own backyard. I was counting on an Indian summer. It was already September. Ruby and I had been back in school three days. My father had said it didn't make sense filling the pool this time of year. I knew he was right when he told me that, at best, we'd only get a couple of weeks' use out of it. It wouldn't be worth the chemicals we'd have to pour in. But I played up the fact that I was turning fourteen in a couple of days. I'd never had a birthday without a swim in the pool. It was a family tradition, I said. But I could tell he wanted to see if all the work Uncle Günter had put in down there had paid off.

I turned on the hose the night before my birthday. The pool was half full by morning. That afternoon we prepared my trout on the barbecue. We'd cleaned them and put them in the freezer the night we got home from the lake, because nobody had felt like cooking . We ate hamburgers along with the fish and, for dessert, an apple crisp with fourteen blue and red candles stuck in the top. I made a wish and blew once as hard as I could. The flames lowered like sails under a hard wind, tipped, and drowned in a lake of brown sugar. But one remained upright. I licked my finger and thumb, prepared to snuff it out, but Günter quickly leaned over the table and blew it down.

After lunch, around mid-afternoon, we staged another mini-Olympics. Ruby and I put our bathing suits on. Our somersaults over the grass that day were as high as they had ever been. Monika called out scores along with my parents while Uncle Günter sat and watched. On my hands I walked from the rock garden to the deck, up onto the diving board, and held the handstand a moment longer. I focused on my thumbs, waited a moment longer, hunched my shoulders, and slid smoothly, finally, into the cold water. The pool reached around my body like a live animal and squeezed me into a tight ball. When I opened my eyes I saw the faint blue traces of my uncle's repairs crawling up the sloping sides of the pool like rivers on a map.

I dared Ruby to jump in that day. "You'll get used to it," I told her, splashing outwards with an open palm. She stood on the diving board, a game of ours from the summer before, playing it up for the adults as they sat at the picnic table, drinking their coffee and apple schnapps. She took a running jump and arced through the air, hanging against the real sun, my little sister, the future gymnast, and broke the water with a delighted screech. Monika smiled and raised her schnapps over her head. From the water I saw my uncle leave the picnic table.

After dinner we turned on the TV for the first time in two days. So far Canada had only won three bronze and a silver. We were hoping for news of gold. The Games were closing soon. We didn't have much time. At nine o'clock we settled in the TV room to watch the day's highlights. Ruby in the beanbag, my mother with her knitting, my father leafing through *Wind and Sail*. News footage lit up the room. First a shot of an airport, then masked men and a helicopter. Monika was sitting in the rocking chair beside Ruby. Uncle Günter came in from the front porch, where he'd been sitting with his back against a pillar, reading a copy of *Stern* since dinner. I made a space for him on the couch. I felt the heat come off him when he sat down and his thigh brushed against me.

"You're from there," Ruby said, grabbing Monika's hand when she heard the voice-over say Fürstenfeldbruck. The Munich Olympiad had been suspended today at three-forty-five, the announcer said. The Israeli team was withdrawing. Günter leaned forward, the magazine rolled in his hand.

There was a shot of flags flying at half mast. His eyes rolled back into his head like they'd done the day he inhaled the dry dusty earth of my mother's garden. Then the voice-over again. Eleven Israelis had been killed, a Munich sergeant, and five terrorists. My mother's hands fell open. Pictures of a stockinged face peering around a corner came on. As the scene played out, my mother translated for her brother. Her voice softly floating beneath the glow of the screen. Günter's face didn't change. Ruby didn't understand what the announcer was saying.

"What does hostage mean? What's *hostage!*"

"Prisoner," I said. Then the footage of more men in masks, a man throwing a hand grenade into a helicopter as it sat on the tarmac, its still propellers hanging low to the ground like the branches of the tree I'd stood under while watching Monika. There was a moment's pause before it exploded, a room-filling yellow the same as the rays of sun I'd seen at the lake before my uncle's arm pulled me back to the surface.

"*Juden!*" my uncle said, slapping his thigh. He rolled his fish eyes back around from the inside of his head towards me, as if I was to understand something that no one else could. He laughed something else in German I didn't get and drummed the rolled-up magazine down against my thigh. My mother shot her head around to him and looked at him icily. Didn't he own me now? I thought. His hand was warm on my leg.

"Okay, that's enough," my mother said angrily and scooped the ball of wool from her lap. She put down her knitting needles, took Ruby by the wrist, and marched her up to her room. "I don't *want* to be a *Juden*," I heard her call as she stomped her feet up the stairs beside my mother. "Don't *you* treat me like a *Juden!*"

My mother came back down a few minutes later. She didn't say anything. She looked at her brother. I could see she was furious. My father put his hands on his knees, about to step between them, his wife and his brother-in-law. Monika was ready to speak. Then I saw something in her eyes that told me this was between brothers and sisters. Not husbands and wives. Not Israelis and Germans and Palestinians. This was about the salt that had pervaded their lives and drained the life from their father, kept the scent of death from the door that June in 1944. This was about cattle cars and blizzards. This was about the heart of my family. Monika was not blood. She would have her turn at him upstairs, alone. Somewhere else, but not here. I watched my mother. I saw her thinking, her fists clasped. I wondered if she could hit someone. Then I saw tears come up in her eyes and she turned and left the room and went back upstairs. Monika got up and walked out onto the porch. My father turned off the TV and told me to get to bed. I closed my bedroom door behind me and sat on the edge of my bed and imagined Ruby across the hall drawing the word *hostage* in the air with a finger.

Sometime around midnight I got up to pee. I stood over the sound of spilling water, still half asleep, and thought about what my uncle was leaving behind for us—a full pool, a wound in the earth shining in the moonlight. I knew this is how we'd have to leave things. The vacation was over. They were leaving tomorrow.

I went downstairs, through the kitchen and into the dark sunroom that opened onto the backyard, and found Günter in the pool. From the doorway I watched him swim, his long arms powering him through the water, back and forth like a man pacing the length of a small room. I walked out onto the damp grass and crouched in the shadows by the rock garden. For an hour and more I waited like that, expecting him to go under. I pulled a piece of crabgrass from the lawn and sucked the stalk while I watched his darkened figure move through the water. Then I felt the first drop of rain to fall in eight weeks, a light sprinkle, and then the sky swirled and it began to pour. The pool jumped alive and bubbled. I stabbed my tongue into the warm rain, savouring the end of our drought, and formed a cup with my hands. Günter stopped in the middle of the pool and called something out to me then. But I didn't answer. What if he'd passed something on to me? I thought. I couldn't move. What if, at the lake, my life had passed into his hands when he pulled me from the water? I heard him call out my name again in a way I'd never heard my name spoken before, a weak fearing voice that carried the secrets I'd never know. I waited like that and listened, the rain on my skin and face beading as the voice called for me again and again through the dark, and finally I raised my cupped hands to my lips and drank.

III

———◦《◎》◦———

Willy tapped a cane over the cement floor, his eyes rolling in their sockets like heavy wet stones. A roar of applause groaned down through the walls from the open cup of stadium above his head. The torch was being carried through the main gate, he imagined. Behind his glistening stone eyes he imagined a white cloud of doves rising to the sky. As he considered this, the larger of two boys leaning up against the groaning wall kicked the cane out from under the hobbling man and laughed when he fell. "Jews and cripples not allowed," the boy yelled. He gently nudged the man with his boot. "*Verstehst Du?*"

GOLEM

NEXT SUMMER AS we drive down through the foothills of Bavaria, receding blue mountain to left and right, my mother tells us about the cloud of mustard gas that redesigned Willy's nervous system way back during the First World War. It's bad and getting worse, she says. That's why we're visiting now, while we still can. Somewhere north of Munich she leans back over her seat, left elbow pointing between Ruby and me as we listen. I hear the hesitation in her voice when the part about the gas comes up. Maybe she's thinking about her father, something they had between them before he died.

"Uncle Willy was there for the fraternization incident," she says. "That's what they called it." This is the Christmas Eve night in the first year of the war when the British stopped firing on Willy and his friends, and Willy and his friends stopped bombing the British. The Christmas when time stopped. My mother tells us he got two goals and an assist playing soccer the next morning on the field they'd cleared between the two front lines. For a moment she stops talking and looks out the window at the blue of the mountains. She puts on her thinking face. I watch her quarter profile, an eye moving with the contours of the roadside. My father's flipping through the channels on the radio when we enter the side of a mountain, a long dark hole, and burrow deep into the earth. Car headlights pass us in the opposite lane and I think of my mother's father dying in a salt mine, the brother of the man we're on our way to see. Outside in the open again, a bright Sousa march suddenly jumps out from American Forces Radio. My mother leans forward and turns it off.

"Right away, from the moment it touched his skin," she says, "his body grew a mind of its own. It didn't do what he wanted it to." She's back to talking about the gas. Between thought and action, she says, there was a moment's pause after the poison touched his skin, a dormancy, like the space between the voice and its echo in a deep canyon. This is how I imagine it as she tells us. He feels the delay, the command cascading along his veins before it enters the world through his fingertips, or is breathed into the world on the lips. The moment when the rest of the world seems to fall still and silent. She says her uncle was returned from the war with nothing at all, not a scratch, no wound but the suggestion of simpleness, the air of a man who struggles with the idea of breath before getting down to the business of breathing.

We've been on the road for two weeks now. I've seen my mother cry tears of joy while handling the gold-knit tapestry of the handmaids of King Ludwig II at Schloss Herren-Chiemsee, the island castle accessible only by boat where my grandparents got married back in 1936 after they met at the Olympics. We've walked through the Black Forest and had our portraits painted in the main square in Cologne. My father has played pick-up accordion with a high school friend in Frankfurt. I've placed my hand against the Berlin Wall and wondered who was telling the truth, us or them. As we drive between cities in the Opel my father bought second-hand at a garage in Amsterdam, Ruby and I keep our eyes peeled for deer grazing along the Autobahn and the skinny men with beards who stand at the on-ramps with their thumbs in the air, pointing upwards, as if that's where they want to go. In the game we invent to help pass the time, a deer is worth five times that of a man. I keep score because Ruby is too young to understand the rules. She's eleven. I'll be going into grade ten in the fall.

"It's like looking at movie film without the projector," my mother says, turning back to face the highway again, the clicking of her knitting needles starting up over her lap. She's working on a fall sweater for me. "That's how he explained it to me when I was your age. The clunking movements."

We spend hours at a time in the car. The knitting grows louder up front when my mother's understanding of her uncle's life draws silence. And when my parents disagree about stopping, which is most of the time. Maybe it's just being back in the German world that's affecting my mother this way. The weight of the pavement a few inches beneath our feet fills the car with the illusion of purpose and destination. Sometimes my father drives with the radio on, tuned to a station that plays out the American music we all know, something that binds us, a something we can all sink our teeth into.

My father and I don't mind the driving. We're used to it from our storm-hunting when we spend whole days in the car searching out tornadoes. This visit to the Old World will cut into our severe weather season, I think. But for a time the trade-off seems fair. Until my mother's sick uncle comes into the picture. By mid-morning my mother and Ruby begin pestering my father to pull over. They want to get out and stretch their legs. The few times there hasn't been anyone to stay with, we've slept in bed and breakfasts. When it comes to that my father calls ahead. But usually we stay in the cramped apartments of their old school friends. In the north, a high school chum of my father's showed us fistfuls of money from the Weimar Republic and told Ruby and me that back in his father's day a wheelbarrow of the stuff didn't buy you a loaf of bread.

I don't question my father's need to drive. I'd rather be back home scouring the province for tornadoes or stuffing my pockets with chocolate bars at the back of Ramsey's Drugs or fishing the Joshua for black bass and catfish. But the sheer volume of road seduces me. The world, I'm finding, does not end. I don't care where we go. Ruby suffers car sickness and takes little white pills to ease her stomach. Sometimes she lays her head on my lap. I wiggle my toes to stop the pins and needles and tap my father on the shoulder. Then I lean forward and whisper in his ear that Ruby needs to stop, maybe it's a good idea to pull over next chance we get. We're half an hour from Fürstenfeldbruck. After a pee-break we climb back in. Ruby's sitting up now, refreshed, less nauseated. My mother starts knitting again. For a time only the clicking of the needles fills the car. Ruby's looking out her window for deer, eager to catch up. I'm winning, ten to two. Then the needles stop and my mother turns around in her seat.

"I only told you about the gas so you won't make a big deal about it." She looks at me, her eyebrows raised. "Got it?"

"Roger dodger," I say, and it occurs to me that this is the summer I'm going to play tricks on my mother's sick uncle.

"I'm serious," she says. Then to Ruby: "Don't ask Uncle Willy any funny questions, okay, honey?"

"Where do Germans keep their armies?" she sings, rubbing her eyes with the small heels of her palms. She's heard this one from me. She says it a hundred times a day now. She can't wait for the answer. "In their sleevies!" she screeches and laughs.

"I mean the other funny, remember? *Strange* questions about how he moves. Remember it's not polite to stare."

"You heard your mother, *Junge,*" my father says, looking at me in the rear-view mirror. "No wisecracks." He winks, then starts in on a long bend.

"There's one! There's one!" Ruby shouts. "Deers!"

Willy must be in his mid-seventies. A great grinding question mark hooks under the skin of his back. They stand on the sloping grass beside the farmhouse. Willy leans on a mahogany cane. My mother stoops and hugs him. They're talking quickly in Bayrisch, the Bavarian dialect unknown to my father. He waits respectfully, a little off to the side, until they switch back into German. He's never met Willy before. None of us has except my mother. He wants to keep driving. But I'm thinking maybe he realizes we've been on the road too much lately, that he's been pushing his luck. When he sees a tear run down my mother's cheek he knows this rolling vacation's got to come to a screeching halt. I see him shoring up his resolve. Ruby stands in the open wing of the car door, twirling her hair in her fingers, something she does when she's sleepy. The country air is heavy with the shade of cattle. I look up the sides of the valley. There's nothing here but this house, alpine-looking, like a Bavarian postcard. Milking cows pause on the shadowing afternoon hills to gaze at us on the path below.

"Here is my favourite son," my mother says brightly in German, brushing her cheek with a sleeve. Willy's face is narrow. A thin man, not much of a farmer, I think. I imagine his mind reach out before his arm moves to shake my extended hand. The delay is still there. It's more than just a shyness. I remember the story we learned in class of the Archduke Ferdinand's assassination. By all accounts, the unnecessary war. The war Willy fought. I wait. His shoes point outwards, like a clown's. They're on the wrong feet. I want to withdraw my hand, to step back from him. I want to get back in the car and keep driving. I want to look for storms. His hand drifts up between us like an afterthought, a smile drifts slowly across his face. I'm shaking hands with a war wound.

His voice has an old man's timbre. He's saying something to me.

"*Grüss Gott*," I answer.

"He says you look just like me," my mother says, translating.

I release his grip and step aside. Ruby shakes his hand like a young adult, unfazed.

"We saw deer from the road," she says, grinning. It doesn't matter that he can't understand her. Awkwardly he reaches to her small head and tousles her hair.

From a distance I study Willy's tic while the grown-ups sit around the kitchen table drinking coffee and eating poppy-seed cake. Ulla, his housekeeper, sits with us. The whole conversation's in German. Ruby and I sit politely. We clean our plates and wait for our mother to pour out more fresh milk into our glasses. With my rough under-standing of German I gather Ulla lives on the farm, a live-in nursemaid in this one-man sanatorium. No one says anything about her husband. Or maybe I've missed something. I sip at my milk and wonder if Willy has been married, if anybody ever consented to him. Ulla cuts the corner of the cake with her fork, takes a mouthful, and rises from her chair. Still chewing broadly, she returns from the refrigerator with three white containers and counts out a handful of colourful pills. The table falls silent. When she finishes she pushes them over to Willy and he swallows each, one by one, his milky eyes turned to the ceiling. His hands like claws. He rolls each pill into the small scoop of an unclipped fingernail and lifts it to his mouth like a crane, his wrist pointing outwards. Ruby's feet paddle under the table nervously until our mother releases us from the kitchen.

We run outside, filling our lungs with air. In the barn I climb up into the rafters while Ruby waits down below. Sparrows dart in and out through spaces between the boards. Dust pauses in the shafts of light entering through cracks in the old walls. Harnesses and wooden crates and dusty skis piled on the thick pine beams above our heads.

"Watch this," I say, affecting a horrible body spasm. "It's Uncle Spaz." I leap into the air and fall twisting, my tongue sticking out the side of my mouth. I come up from the haystack, covered in straw and dust. "Uncle Super Spaz is going to get you." I lurch towards my sister like a hungry Frankenstein, lead-footed. "I'm going to give you the Mustard Brain disease if you don't run," and she takes off through the open barn door, screaming with delight. Her footsteps run across the compound towards the house and the kitchen door swings open and slams shut.

That first night, after supper, my mother and Willy sit apart from us. They linger at the kitchen table while the rest of us settle into other parts of the house. There's no sign of the laughing I've come to expect of these summer nights with relatives and friends. Instead, from the kitchen comes the hushed talking, the unintentioned clink of a spoon against china. My father's accordion remains tucked away in the trunk of the car.

Ulla goes upstairs. In the living room my father and I study maps of Europe. His eye and finger speed along red and black highways to parts of the country we haven't been yet. I'm kneeling beside him. He traces down into Italy, France, and Spain.

"We'll see all of these places," he says. Then, "Look at this." He pulls the map closer to him over the hardwood floor. "The great seaports and rivers of Europe. See how all the important towns are collected along the rivers and natural harbours. Here and here and here," he says, pointing to Bremen, then London, then Barcelona. I lean closer. "This is where we were last week," indicating the small blue dot near Hanover where we rented a sailboat while Ruby and my mother walked in the trees along the shoreline.

Beside us Ruby sits talking to herself. A family of dolls spread out before her, presents from Uncle Helmut and his wife in Frankfurt. I got a boomerang and a drafting set. She picks up the baby doll. "This is Gertrude," she says to herself. "But she doesn't mind when you call her 'Bertha,' either." Then there's a soft moan from the kitchen, like the sound of a child blubbering. My father looks over his shoulder. His finger curls in the middle of the Danube.

Ruby and I are assigned a spare bedroom with a view looking up to the mountains. But by the time we get in there to sleep, it's too dark to see. I sleep on the cot my father's brought up from the basement. It smells musty, like rain and earth and snails. Before the lights go out I notice the wallpaper, green and red cartoon horses standing like people, holding each other around the waist. The checked curtains blow into hollow mouths over the open window. After the lights go out I think about Willy. I imagine a yellow gas caught in his lungs, playing his limbs like a marionette's. I think about the handful of medicine he took at the supper table. I wonder if his pills have anything to do with us. A cuckoo clock ticks over Ruby's bed, on the wall that separates my parents' room from ours. I think about the story my mother told us on the drive here. How Willy fought in the war, and the Christmas Eve truce when time stopped. Before I fall asleep I hear talking coming from my parents' room. But I don't hear what it is they're saying. I dream about horses stuck in mud up to their chests, unfathoming eyes turned upward.

The next day after breakfast we hike up the side of the valley. We stop to rest often, for Willy mostly. But for my mother and Ruby, too. Not because they're tired but because they keep wandering off the trail to pick the blue bell-like *Enzian* that grow over these mountains. My father carries the picnic basket in his right hand, his camera looped around his neck. It's a hot day and he's not saying much. When Ruby and my mother disappear into the woods for the first time, he grows a pained look on his face. He looks over to the opposite side of the valley and snaps some shots, then sits down on a rock and waits. He fiddles with his camera and looks at his watch. I know he's thinking about the part of the country we're not going to be able to see because of this stopover, the storms we'll miss back home. He wants to get in the Opel. He wants to see castles and shipyards. His people no longer live here. His father's back in Kingston, himself now an immigrant like my parents in the only place I know. He can still visit friends here. He likes seeing his old buddies from school. He hasn't seen them for years. But it's not the same. He's got new friends, a new life somewhere else.

Willy leans on his cane. I'm waiting a short distance up the trail. When Ruby and my mother finally come out from the trees, Ruby runs over to Willy and gives him a flower. He blushes and spins in a slow clumsy circle, smiling, and says, "Danke schön, Kanada." As we ascend we turn our heads to watch the valley deepen below. It takes us two hours to get to the top. I keep running ahead, thinking I'll have a better chance at discovering a deer posing among the pine trees if I forge on alone, without the chatter of a clumsy hiking party and the click of an old man's walking stick. I double back, panting. Ruby's holding Willy's elbow as they walk, prattling on to him in English. He smiles, understanding nothing.

When we reach the top Willy leans over and says into my ear: "Say something. Yell something." My German's just good enough. He wants an echo. He wants to show me how his brain works, how the gas feels inside. The farm's a brown dot at the far end of the valley. The laneway we drove over yesterday snakes its way over the green valley floor and disappears behind a hill where it meets up with the road that leads eventually to Munich. He leans back on his cane and waits, Ruby's flower wilting in his fine skeletal hand. For a moment there's only our breathing and the snapping eye of my father's camera.

"Which way's the Berlin Wall?" I ask my father.

"East," he says, without removing his eye from the viewfinder.

Willy gestures to our right, beyond the farm, makes a small pointing circle with his cane. He's heard the word "Berlin."

"*Wunderbar,*" my mother says under her breath. She's looking in the direction of France. Ruby's holding the bouquet of deep-blue flowers they've taken from the woods. Willy leans into my ear again.

"What will you say?" he asks. I taste his old man's breath, notice white stubble on his chin. I wonder at the depth of his illness. Will he die while we're still guests in his house? A grunt of expectation comes from his throat.

With all my might.

"Help!"

The echo draws back over us from the other side. My lungs

burn. My father, at first startled, looks pleased. My mother turns around quickly and looks at me. My voice returns to me weakly from the other side, changed somehow, a bridge of voices crisscrossing over the valley floor. Willy's smiling, his demonstration complete.

At night we sit outside on folding wooden chairs and watch the shadows lengthen over the hills. The evening consumes the new black hair on the shins of my outstretched legs. Ruby's at the foot of the picnic table, warming up. When she's ready, she stands before us and begins a simplified version of the floor routine she's been working on since last winter. A series of front and back handsprings, cartwheels, and somersaults. Even now, after supper and in the fading evening light, she moves like a dancer does, as soundlessly and quick as the bats feeding low in the air over our heads.

My mother holds Willy's hand as they watch the routine. I wonder if he knows what's going on. He's filled up on those pills again. I imagine they've brought him back to where he wants to be, thinned the yellow cloud in his lungs. As Ruby spins through the air I slip around to the back of the house and down into the basement where my mattress comes from. It's dark down here, but I find the light switch and begin looking around. There's a wall of jam jars to the right of the stairs. I want to find something to take home with me. An old gun from the war, a bayonet or hand grenade. Old soldiers keep things like that. I pick up one of the jars from the shelf and brush off the dust with my sleeve. Windfall. I peer through the warped glass and see two pickled lizards. There are dozens of jars, within each a snake or turtle or a few mice or small birds, at least a pair of unhatched eggs or frozen amber-tinged insects. Every jar has a date marked on a piece of tape stuck to the lid: *24 Juni 1958; 17 August 1943; 4 Oktober 1969.* The oldest from April of 1931. The animals hang in a clear copper-coloured liquid. Sediment churns around the tail of a salamander, the swirl of an escaping fish. I open it and sniff in the fumes, rich and sweet, like the fumes of an outboard motor.

On Friday we drive down to Munich to see the Olympic stadium. Willy comes with us. Earlier I heard my parents talking about whether or not he should come. My father said he wanted to make it a family affair. I know he doesn't want to wait for the old-man steps. My mother reminded him he was family, then walked away briskly, arms crossed over her chest.

The stadium's bigger than it looked on TV last year. Ruby

says she'll do her floor routine in a place as grand as this someday. The Montreal Games are only three years away. Enormous concrete ribs arch over our heads and meet at a single point stories above.

"It's like walking into a whale," Ruby says, pointing to the circle of sky above our heads. "That's the blowhole." On the track below two black men practise take-off on the starting blocks. USA is printed in red, white, and blue on the backs of their tracksuits. An older white man stands on the grass beside the runners and fires a pistol at the blue sky through the blowhole. I don't recognize the moment's pause between the shot and the runners' reactions. But they're already up and running when Willy finally flinches at the noise of the gun firing.

After the stadium we walk around the centre of Munich, taking pictures, poking our heads into the silent air of cathedrals. I place my hands on the Madonna's crying cheeks, cool as a river. In the bright sunlight our mother points to things she hasn't seen in years, the green tree-filled parks and pathways that have turned into banks and insurance companies since she was a girl. In Marienplatz, the main square, we drink lemonade and buy mustard-covered pretzels as big as my father's hand. To eat them we sit at the edge of the Fischbrunnen fountain, our five backs to a statue of a spitting carp. According to the lore about this place, a couple of *Pfennig* tossed into the water behind us will make us rich someday. My father digs in, hands me and Ruby one coin each. Ruby throws hers in and bounces up and down, her eyes closed in mighty prayer. I fight the urge to whip mine at the carp and finally launch it off my thumb and watch it hit the water and flutter to the bottom. I sit in the shade my father casts, the fountain's mist cooling my sunburned neck. Willy sits to my left, silently.

My father's already snapped some photos of us standing in front of the fountain. Now he asks an American lady to shoot us and takes a spot beside my mother. The woman holding my father's Nikon looks like the blonde woman on "The Dick Van Dyke Show." Behind the camera she chews a purple hunk of gum, taking her time as she fits the five of us into this single moment in time. "Cheese," she says finally and in unison we reply. A second later Willy's voice joins our photograph, weak and in another language.

"Your mother's part of the country isn't the only interesting part of Germany," my father says quietly, his hand on my moist neck. "How about we go somewhere with water? More water than this fountain. Maybe even the Mediterranean. You've never sailed on salt water. It keeps the boat higher. It's more buoyant." I know my mother's listening. She doesn't say anything. I see her looking at Willy. He's looking at the cane between his knees. But I can't help wondering. I want to taste salt water.

That night I hear crying through the bedroom wall. Ruby's already asleep. I listen to the hard words I remember from last summer when my mother's brother came to visit us in Canada; then the whispers and low tones my mother shared with Willy the first night here around the kitchen table. Then silence, and the sound of crickets returns.

"Come on," I say, leading Ruby down the stairs to the basement. We've already been here three days. My father's taken to washing the car every afternoon in anticipation of our release. My mother waits hand and foot on Willy. Ulla likes us being here. It gives her someone to talk to. She and my mother cook together and go for long walks in the pasture when Willy takes his afternoon nap, the time of day Ruby and I are told to be quiet around the house. I've been coming down here every day to check on the jam jars. They're dust-free now, wiped clean on pant legs and shirts. The light of the single bulb hanging from the rafters holds the small animals in trumpet-coloured suspension.

"Take this one," I say. "And this one. Can you carry three?"

"I can carry more than you," Ruby says. It's after dark now. The grown-ups are around front sitting in the folding chairs. "Take as many as you can but don't drop them or you'll get the Mustard Brain disease."

"But they're dead little things," she says.

There are seven jars between us. We walk over the compound, past the Opel. Its rims shine in the moonlight, the waiting getaway car. The barn emerges like a silent train from the dark, a blacker shape against the grey night. We walk downhill without talking, the jars pressed against our chests. There's the sound of our footsteps against the touch of darkness and small waves riding against the lids of our jars.

"It's okay here," I say. "Put them down." I fumble in my pocket, take out the pack of matches. "You're not going to say anything. Promise again. Remember that Mom and Dad hate tattlers." I wait for her complicity before I show her the matches. I strike one between us and her face appears before me as though slipped out from between black curtains. She doesn't say anything. I throw the match down to the ground, the curtains close again over her face.

"These'll burn good," I say, unscrewing the lid of the first jar. The smell of gasoline. "Spaz-head won't even notice them gone." I pour the contents over the ground. "It's just dead animals."

I tell Ruby to stand back. "Okay. Where are you now?" I ask carefully. I want to make sure her voice is far enough away and that the rest of the jars are a safe distance from the dampened grass. "Get ready," I say, then strike the match and wait a moment for it to flare, watch the flame begin to crawl down the stick. In one motion I step back and throw the match over the puddle and a low blue carpet of fire spreads at our feet, peels the darkness away from Ruby's face beside me. In the middle of the flame one of Willy's dead things shows its teeth. Hisses at the little pyro I've become. We do the seven jars slowly, methodically, like criminals disposing of the evidence. When we're finished I return the empty jars to the basement. The perfect crime.

The next day before breakfast I go and check out the fire pit. It's a big black scar on the grass. A chemical smell hangs in the air. Not all the bones have disintegrated. I nudge them with a stick and make out a small claw. But the vandalism is off the beaten track, well away from Willy's daily wanderings. I could burn a car out here and get away with it.

After lunch we find the stacks of money. Piles of it in the barn loft. Old notes from before the First World War. There must be millions' worth. The rich promise of the fountain in Munich. But I know right away that it's worthless. It's fifty years old, the same stuff Uncle Helmut showed us in Frankfurt, the broad, page-sized notes turned back to paper by hyperinflation after Willy's side lost the war. "You could wipe your bum with it," Uncle Helmut had whispered in my ear and laughed.

"What can we do with it?" Ruby says.

"We can set up a bank," I say, turning a bundle over in my hand. "We can make our own country and make a bank. This is our official currency." We're both kneeling in the loft, a group of pigeons on the highest beam above us, looking down and cooing demurely. The boxes we've cleared away are scattered around us. We count notes the whole morning. I get a calculator from the glove compartment of the car. Our eyes get sore and the batteries run dry just under eight million Reichsmark. We play at buying boats and houses and small islands off the California coast. I have a house in the middle of the Golden Gate Bridge. I buy an airplane. I buy my school back home and fire all the teachers. Ruby lives on a ranch on

Pluto with a pool full of dolphins and sea lions. She makes friends with them and hires all the best scientists in the universe to discover their secret language and teach it to her.

At supper we sit with the dignity that comes easily to the incredibly rich. We are millionaires. We own entire planets. We smile at one another, kick each other under the table when the other starts to laugh. We're on the verge of exploding. If the secret ends, our wealth evaporates. We both know that Ruby's the one who's going to give it away, sooner or later. She can't control herself when it comes to this kind of game. This is a fun secret. The other kind, the burning-dead-animals kind is not a fun secret. But our mirth flies out the window when Ulla rolls Willy's pills out in front of him. They lie there, little robins' eggs, perfect blue pebbles. I feel like winging them across the room with a flick of a finger, beaning my father in the chest or clacking one against the window above the sink. This is our fifth day here, but none of us is comfortable with this ritual. Willy forms a colourful circle with his medicine and begins to work backwards. His clawed finger is the minute hand of a clock ticking in reverse. He starts at eleven. The claw rises, twisted fingernail, drops the pill onto his tongue, swallows. Sip of tea. Ten, nine, eight, all the way round the face of the clock, one after another. My mother has stopped trying to divert us. We sit still except for Ulla, who continues on with her meal, unmoved. My father rolls his eyes, shrugs his shoulders at me. I know where he wants to be. He wants to be on the wind somewhere off the coast of France sailing with a pack of dolphins or playing his accordion with his band back home. But my mother wants to stay put. I have to try harder, she says. "Spend time with Willy," she said the second day. "He's the last I have." I'd heard her say to my father that she didn't want to see her brother, living only a few dozen kilometres from here. She said she wasn't ready to meet him again after last summer. After she saw what he turned out to be.

"I have no one left," she said to me. "Just Willy and he won't be here forever."

"But I don't speak German."

"That's an excuse. Your German's fine. You'll regret it when you're older." She placed her hand on my neck and kissed my forehead.

My father's people are the ones who say the past is passed. You can't go back. And you shouldn't try. We saw what happened two summers ago, when my father's parents wanted to get remarried to celebrate their anniversary and nothing went right. Leave well enough alone. But this is my mother's turn at it. She's giving it a go. Digging for artifacts. Maybe my dad's just trying to save her from the inevitable. Maybe he's learned his lesson. His father lost a wife in the trying.

"You can't change things now," I hear him say softly through the bedroom wall the night after the arson. "You've got to let him go. Let's go to Valencia. There's still time. I'll learn how to say 'I love you' in Spanish." I imagine him on the other side of the bedroom, down on one knee, holding my mother's hand.

The next day Ulla comes into the kitchen with news of the fire, charred bones in a black swath of grass. My mother's peeling potatoes, her wedding band removed and placed safely off to one side of the sink. Later she translates Ulla's story for me, laughing. It's part of farm life, she says. Everyone here has their own stories. She tells me Ulla thinks there are aliens around these parts that come zipping down from the sky in the dark. One landed behind the barn last night or the night before. No, she didn't see it but there's a big round black spot in the pasture where it touched down to do experiments on the cows.

At least one of us is looking ahead, I think, imagining to the time we get off this planet.

"There's another legend here," my mother tells me, still

half-smiling with thoughts of aliens in Bavaria. "They say a golem wanders the mountains, up higher than we went on Tuesday. Do you know what a golem is?"

"No," I say. "Like monster?"

She tells of a man of mud and clay made by a rabbi to protect his people from persecution. He had special powers. But something went wrong and he turned on his people after saving them many times and the peasants forced him out of their town. Now he wanders alone up past the last trails, eating rabbits and crying himself to sleep at night.

"Anything strange they find up there, they blame the golem. Aliens are starting to get dumped on too."

When Ulla rushes back into the kitchen five minutes later and says she needs help, my mother unties her apron, slips the ring back on her finger, and leaves with her through the side door. I follow close behind, down the hill to the site of our cremation, and find my mother kneeling in front of Willy, wiping his face with a handkerchief. Ulla's standing a few feet off to the side. He's sitting in one of the fold-up chairs, his legs stretched out in front of him. He's dug up his old uniform from somewhere. He's got on the paraphernalia I was looking for when I found the jars in the basement—the helmet tilted back on his head, puttees wound around his calves and ankles. A small damp spot of urine grows down the side of his leg. He's just sitting there, staring down at the fire pit, his booted feet crossed lightly at the edge of a circle of tiny bones.

Next morning, when my father opens our bedroom door and says my name, I know it's to say we're leaving. No one talks while we pack up the car. We've wolfed down our breakfast and watched Willy take his medicine for the last time. My father's convinced us of the necessity of salt water. We're going to rent a sailboat near Valencia and sail with those packs of dolphins. In a better world, the one of aliens and sea lions on Pluto, my sister would speak with these animals for us, ask them where we can find the prettiest coral at the bottom of the sea. *What do you do in those vast fields of watery space?* she would ask. But we don't speak their language and I don't speak Willy's language and the old man doesn't know the only world I know back home. We are all isolated, cut off from each other despite my mother's attempts to bring us together, to meld our three generations. My father's not being bull-headed. He's trying to hold us together, to save us.

They're all standing around the Opel. I emerge from the barn with a pocketful of old Reichsmark, blinking in the morning sun. I've already packed away some of Willy's jars. Souvenirs of my summer back in the Old World. The car doors hang open. Ruby's quiet, too, like my mother, thinking about the day ahead of us and our parents' silence and the click of the knitting needles to come.

My father extends his hand to Willy and I watch his body played cruelly like a marionette and the arm rise slowly to meet my father's hand. They shake twice, my father's grip more powerful, decisive. Then he kisses Ulla on the cheek and, patting his stomach, says something about cakes and they both laugh sadly. My mother's determined not to cry. She hugs Willy and they stand motionless for a good minute until my sister calls out.

"Come on," she says, annoyed now by this grown-up solemnity. "We've got to look for *deers.*" She's already said her goodbyes. She's standing in the open door. I shake Ulla's hand and step sideways to Willy, hold out my hand and wait for the drifting gesture of his wound, this last touch. I feel the sun on my forehead. But his hand disappears into his pocket. He seems to carve out something in there, gently manoeuvring, searching within the deep warm cave of his baggy pants. My mother shifts, Ulla crosses her arms over her breasts. My father looks across the laneway that will lead us out of here. Then Ruby climbs into the back seat and watches this happen through the rear window, like she's glimpsing a deer at the side of a highway perform some impossible human gesture, something closer to compassion and forgiveness than the woods have ever known. But we all see this. We all watch as the dying uncle brings out for me a small living animal, a barn swallow. He holds it in his thin, clawed fingers against my face. I feel it, the brush of beak and feather, small heart racing.

IV

—⊷«◉»⊶—

Lottie stood at the lip of the ten-metre platform. She saw the dive in her mind one last time, a second self launch into air, assuming the pike position, one and a half rolls and straightening again like a spear to enter water. Silke waited in the stands with her camera at the ready. She watched her friend shift on the platform above her. She watched her open her arms, then gently rise up onto her toes. A wind carried clouds across the sun. There was the sound of the churning water below. The two women concentrated silently, unaware of the poorly dressed German sailor just down from where Silke sat ready with her camera. By the time Lottie entered water he had imagined their life together through to the end.

RUBY

When She Flew

ONE DAY IN May of 1978 while I trained, face down in the warm chlorinated water of Centennial Public Pool, I remembered the history of my sister's illness and her constant need to fly. Ruby was the charity of my choice. She had been in remission now for almost a year. In a week's time I would attempt to remain in water without touching the sides or bottom of the pool longer than anyone had ever done before me. All donations would go to cancer research. Drown proofing was not new to me. I'd taught myself after the summer I nearly drowned at Kelso. In the event of an emergency, it was a more efficient use of energy than treading water. Ruby and I called it Dead Man's Float. That day, a week before my record attempt, I slowed down my breathing to a point where I felt light-headed. Swimmers splashed around me. Face down, half in dream, I remembered Ruby's desire to leave the world behind and touch the clouds.

I imagined her held aloft to the light for inspection imme-diately after her birth, opening her arms in the anticipation of flight, hands and fingers arched. Cocked for ascent. Days later in the car on the way home from hospital, I imagined her cupping her hands against the movement of air blowing in through the open window. What this was and how it moved objects she must have already known somewhere deep inside her. All this, maybe from our grandmother, Lottie, the Olympic diver. The first of the family to take to the clouds.

As an infant Ruby would lie in her crib under a floating mobile of snowflakes cut from paper napkins, their sharp cor-ners sagging with August heat, reaching. Outside, chickadees gamed among the maples. On a cloudless day of her first sum-mer, she moved her arms, beat against the mattress, kicked her legs. She craned her neck until tears fanned across her cheek. Her small body complied, rose in flight, and she tast-ed one of those snowflakes on her tongue, suspended five feet above her crib, spinning lazily. Later, she swore it to me like this. Barely three months in this world, she felt air breathe beneath the small of her back as she rose. *I flew that day*, she said to me, *I know because that snowflake was cold!*

There were many stories like that. In 1970 I was the older brother who listened to Ruby tell her stories of levitation and flight. She was convinced. But she had nothing to back up her claim other than the stories my mother recounted at breakfast over our favourite cereal. *At Loblaws yesterday I left Ruby sitting snug in the shopping cart, staring up at the cereal on the top shelf. When I got back a second later the cart was full of Fruitloops. It was overflowing. No one else around to help her up there.* And Ruby, smiling then, pushing her bowl to the centre of the table for more. Or the story of the elastic-powered balsa wood propeller plane that my grandmother gave me. One morning, after it got stuck in the branches of the highest maple on our street, I ran back to the house to fetch our father. When we returned, the ladder clanking between us, we found Ruby holding the plane in her teeth, still moving her arms like a butterfly.

I had no reason not to believe. I had already performed my own small miracle. In the tub one day, after cleaning my knees of grass stains, my ears of wax, I lay back in the water and focused my eyes on the soapy horizon, observing the small rising coast of my body breathe against the lapping tide.

I went under and stayed like that until I felt myself breathe. Underwater, my chest rose and fell, even down there. I believed gills formed on my neck, just below my ears. Looking up through the surface of the water, I wondered at the foreign world of air above, the place my sister inhabited.

We believed we were a gifted family. We were Olympians. No miracle seemed misplaced on us. By that summer, I knew that normal people did not fly, could not breathe underwater. But we did. I believed we were evolving. At night I read to Ruby all the dinosaur books I could find at the Centennial Public Library. We pored over artists' interpretations of the first creatures to take to dry land. Pictures of foraging dinosaurs and the slow erection of man on the evolutionary chart, from monkey-dog to Homo sapien. Beside the last figure, we drew ourselves: a winged angel and a web-footed frogman. Television helped. Captain Kirk, though still able to bleed blood red, floated like a bird through airless seas. He was the triumph of evolution, a reunion of flyer and amphibian. What he was we were quickly moving towards.

The gifts our family possessed were endless then it seemed. My father's sailing ships never sank—never so much as sprang a leak. The clothing my mother sewed for us with fine-boned hands protected us from all weather, including the tornadoes my father and I ventured into. We were always warm and dry, even on the coldest, dampest days. Our grandparents delivered the bushels of ripe fruit they'd plucked from orchards north of Kingston. My father's father cobbled shoes and told Ruby and me you could know a lot about a man from what he wore on his feet. What sort of ground he liked to walk on, where he'd been, where he was likely to go. But we were leaving the earth behind. Already then.

Where they'd been was far away. Germany was an Olympic country. Later we discovered it was a great criminal to be reckoned with, a dumb beast still fumbling in a pool of prehistoric muck. Grateful for the distance between it and ourselves, Ruby and I refused its language. Even when we could not help but understand, we turned blank stares to our mother and father when they spoke to us in German. *Was willst du, Junge? Bist du müde?* The simplest interrogative, the most necessary offer of food, we met with hungry, staring eyes. We were obstinate. After years, they relented. Even our grandparents saw that their efforts were in vain, realized this new language we used between ourselves was air and light. In the end they spoke to us and the new world around them in the strong hard-edged accents of Hollywood-movie villains.

Our first trip to the museum, we watched the evolution of the world. In glass cases we observed bubbling tar pits swallow our ancestors. Uncle Günter, my mother's brother from Germany, came along that day. Ruby and I ran ahead to the next display, the adults, already tired of this visit, walking behind slowly through dark corridors. They'd reverted to their old language. Between my uncle's weak mumblings, the taped cries of pterosaurs echoed from speakers hidden under plastic ferns and hatching plaster-of-Paris eggs. This was Ruby's domain. At the flight exhibit, she reached down into the pen for a fallen albatross feather and placed it in her hair. Our uncle thought she was playing Indian. He said in his broken English, "I am Cowboy," and pretended to ride his horse between a group of Japanese. Sneering, Ruby turned back to the albatross and measured its wingspan against her outstretched arms.

I sought traces of marine life: ichthyosaur and gryodus, creatures bearing a greater resemblance to my family history than this strange uncle from Germany. Their skeletons swam against a wall of rock, bathed in shimmering light that represented a wind played on prehistoric seas. I did not fight the illusion. I imagined diving down there among my predecessors, long-toothed and free. My hands had once resembled the fins of a dolphin.

Already I saw the great distance forming between my sister and me. We were evolving, but in different directions. Everyone else stood still. That day, she ran back to the flight exhibit after seeing the mummy in the Egypt room. I knew the possibility of death had unhinged her. No one had seen her sneak off. "Back this way," my father said, guessing. We followed him to the second floor and found her sitting on the back of the albatross, suspended ten feet in the air by gleaming wires, the feather in her hair, riding the bird as if it were a winged horse.

That was an Olympic summer. Ruby was nine. She'd already seen Olga Korbut reach for the ceiling in Munich. She thought it was all perfectly normal. But as Ruby's talents soared, the gifts my family possessed began to fade. The summer before, my grandmother had died. Now my grandfather was alone in Kingston. The following spring, my father was informed that one of the sailboats he'd designed went down off the southern coast of St. Lucia. I was growing faster than our mother could sew. There was no choice but to wear clothing bought from a store. I was cold and damp the whole winter of 1972.

Ruby started training three days a week at the gym with a part-time gymnastics coach named Sarah. Before long she was competing. That was when my mother started talking about losing a daughter for all the time she spent swinging from the uneven bars, away at meets around the province, sometimes in Quebec and New York and Michigan. In the spring of 1973, Ruby cleaned up at the provincials and got the attention of Boris Bajin, the coach of the national team. He said she had a rare talent. She hung longer in the air than anyone he'd ever coached. A rare ability, he said. There was still time to make her into a world-class gymnast. I went to the gym with her after school and watched her train. Boris stood to one side of the mat she was working over, wringing his hands together, and yelled *harder*, clapped once and arched his back as she let go of the bar. "We're going to have to raise the roof if you go any higher," he said that day.

Then later. "There's talent there," he said sitting at the kitchen table, cutting into the cake that my mother had placed in front of him. "Tremendous talent." My father told him about the Olympic blood in our veins. He showed him pictures of my grandmother and grandfather standing together in Berlin, one of those red-and-black flags and a man in jackboots caught in the background. And his own pictures of Rome.

"Josef," Boris said. He put down his fork and took the Berlin photograph in his hand. "What are we going to do? You know something like this requires commitment."

"Elizabeth?" my father said. My mother was at the sink, rinsing out the coffee filter. Her wedding ring sat on the countertop, a safe distance away from the drain. She turned around, hands still dripping.

"I'm not prepared to lose my daughter to someone else's lost dream."

Boris and my father looked at each other across the table. I knew my father. *Give it time,* his face said, then winked a knowing eye. Boris understood. He gave the picture back to my father and silently returned to his cake.

A week later, my mother took Ruby aside. She held her small calloused palms in her hands and looked at them sadly. "Is this what you want? Leather hands. The hands of a sixty-year-old woman before you're a teenager."

"I want to fly," she answered, and my mother got up from the edge of my sister's bed and left the room in tears. That's what did it for my mother, I think, this turning away from her to something she did not understand. She was not an Olympian. Evolution was not hers. Most of her family had died, been killed in the war, or left to languish among the ruins only to visit here with memories of what she had left behind. But Ruby's was a flight forward, all of us but our mother could see that.

That summer my father and I chased storms more than ever. Like my sister, he also knew the power of wind. There was something practical in how he understood air and wind. I saw it in the way he yearned for tangible results. The uprooting of telephone poles, the movement of forty-foot yachts over weather-chopped water, leaning, bowing to the wind. Nothing thrilled him more than a house expanding and shuddering under the pressure of high winds, or a water-spout dancing over the dark waters of Lake Simcoe, my hand in his, sweating, trying to pull away.

We monitored the Ontario Weather Centre, always on the lookout for severe weather. Tornadoes were our jackpot. Sometimes we'd be gone entire weekends looking for storms. My father took off work when word came in that something was brewing on the horizon. Sometimes we'd drop Ruby off at the gym in Burlington on our way out to the storms. From the car the three of us would wave to my mother on the doorstep as we pulled out of the driveway, the look of sadness and confusion already marked across her forehead, and she would wave back and stand with her arm in the air until we turned at Lakeshore Road and headed west and we could see her no longer.

Next in February 1976 came the national qualifying meet. When she flew. Ruby's new uniform arrived early in the new year. Despite our insisting, she refused to try it on for fear that it carried a spell that wore off with each donning. It was red with white stripes down the side, a small Maple Leaf stitched into the right shoulder. A woman from the local paper came to our house two weeks before she left for the Tate-Mackenzie Gymnasium at York University. She asked my sister what a crack at a medal in Montreal would mean to her. She said her ambition was to fly like she'd seen Olga Korbut do four years earlier in Munich.

The first day of the women's competition we watched her walk across the mats and mingle with the other gymnasts. She bounced up and down on the floor mat a few times, then at the vault, testing the air. The gymnasium was at half capacity. We were near the floor, beside a couple from Red Deer. I told them my sister was down there. "The blonde ponytail," I said, pointing. "In the red suit." As she warmed up, the hair fastened at the back of her head bounced like a bird's wing.

"She must be good," the woman said.

"She can really fly."

My mother was wringing her hands. She'd left the knitting bag she usually carried back home. My father was talking a mile a minute to anyone in earshot, sometimes looking down at his fingers as he fed film into his camera. He leaned across my mother's lap.

"Doesn't she look grand down there," he said to the couple beside me. "Look at her!" and they both nodded generously. "The little Olympian."

Before her first event, Ruby fidgeted on the bench. I knew she was rerunning her routines over and over in her head, perfecting each twist and arch in her mind one last time. I prayed she'd repeat those routines she'd mapped out in her head so perfectly. I watched her small heaving chest fill with anticipation when her number was called. There was flight in her step, more elegant than any of us had ever seen before. Boris smiled, nervously running the zipper of his tracksuit up and down over his chest. He loosened his neck as she walked across the floor. Other events continued around her. She paused at the top of the runway, stepped one foot back, bent a knee, waited, then exploded down the mat. She hit the springboard with a bang and rose to meet the vault, twisting, touched the horse leather, popped once again into air as my father's camera clicked, then nailed a one and a half. She straightened her back and threw her head towards us, smiling.

There were no new medals on the fireplace mantel that winter. She didn't make the team. She was barely thirteen. I reminded her that she'd been training for under four years; she'd gone up against the best in the country. She'd still have a shot at the Moscow Games. She was depressed through the spring and into summer. Sometimes she came out of it. But it would settle over her again, as if she'd lost more than anyone knew. That year brought a warm fall, but Ruby hurried my mother in the preparation of more hand-knit sweaters. "Make it thicker," she'd say of a sweater-in-progress, testing the angora wool against her cheek. She wore my mother's sweaters when the rest of us were still wearing T-shirts. In the heat of that summer she'd sat huddled under a blanket in front of the TV watching the Games unfold in Montreal. Into the third week of an Indian summer, a boy from up the street told me that girls wore baggy clothes to hide their flat chests. That fall Ruby did her homework in front of the fireplace. She went to bed early almost every night.

"She had her hopes up, that's all," my father said. "She just needs time." I heard him talking to Boris on the phone. "I remember feeling like that after Rome, after we were edged out of the medals."

But she was losing strength. It was more than not making the team. She'd taken to sitting out practice. The day of the first snow a teacher called, hinting at family problems.

On a Tuesday in December, back for lunch, I found my mother slouched over at the kitchen table. She got up and held me in her arms. Tears ran on her cheeks. "We were at the doctor's this morning," she said. "Ruby's sick."

I waited a moment. "With what?"

"Ruby's got something wrong with her," she said angrily in a voice that surprised and frightened me. Her left hand started to shake. I took hold of her arm and sat with her. I poured her out some tea. Then she told me what they'd found.

I watched my mother's eyes as she spoke. She was looking around herself for strength. I knew I wasn't what she needed right then. I went to the living room and called my father at work but they told me he was already on his way. I replaced the receiver and went upstairs. Ruby was in her room, sitting upright against the headboard of her bed, the pink duvet my mother had made for her the year before pulled up over her legs.

"Booby?" I took her hand and rubbed the leather pads on

her palms. She was looking out the window at the sparrows in the maple trees. "Tell me the story again about the first time you flew."

Nothing was confirmed until the spinal tap that night. In her hospital room, I held Ruby's hand when the doctor stuck her with the butterfly needle. She already had an IV hooked up to her right arm. She cried out and pulled my arm into her chest. My mother touched her forehead. "It hurts now," my father said, wincing. "But they've got to find out what's wrong." There were coloured posters of Big Bird and Aquaman on the wall across from the bed. I watched the white liquid slowly fill the cylinder the nurse had attached to the needle.

My mother stayed with her in the hospital that night. My father and I drove home in silence. It was before eight when we pulled into the driveway. I went straight to the Centennial Public Library and got out all the books I could find on dinosaurs and the evolution of birds.

The chemo started the next day. Every morning she was given drugs with prehistoric names like vincristine and prednisone. They were trying to get her into remission. "Ruby," I said that first afternoon, *The Riddle of the Dinosaur* cradled in my arm. "You wanna hear about archaeopteryx?" Without waiting for her answer, I sat down beside her on the bed.

" 'Stonecutters in Bavaria'—which is where we were three summers ago—'made one of the most fascinating discoveries of all time.' "

I paused and looked up at Big Bird. Ruby was staring out the window into the trees.

" 'They found the fossil remains of what looked like a reptile, possibly a small dinosaur, that in some respects bore a resemblance to a bird, for it had feathers. Darwin had hypothesized that birds must have developed from reptiles, and there was the evidence, so it seemed, in the reptile-bird known as Archaeopteryx. Evolutionists could scarcely believe their good fortune.' "

After school I visited and read to her about the emergence of flying creatures. She was losing weight fast. Soon most of the veins in her arms had collapsed from the IV. By the end of the first week, the nurses were forced to move to the veins in her feet to hook her up. She had nothing left in her arms. After I read to her about the existence of the archaeopteryx, the bird-reptile, I read to her the accounts of the discoveries of the London, Berlin, Maxburg, Teyler, and Eichstatt specimens. At night I remembered the evolutionary charts we had drawn in, the winged angel she always drew beside my frog-man.

I tried to get her to talk. To bring her out of her pain. To give her somewhere to go.

"It's about us coming back together again," I said. "The same evolutionary path."

After thirteen days of intensive chemo, Ruby came home. She'd lost close to fifteen pounds. There were poke marks in her back from the repeated spinal taps. Her skin looked like the mottled hide of an ankylosaur. Within a month, she ballooned. The vincristine kept her eating all day long. I wondered if I was the only one to see how they were hurting her. I found clumps of hair on her pillow. By evening, transparent blonde balls of hair tumbled across the living-room floor at the slightest push of air. She had sores on her face. The smallest infection could send her back to hospital. Whenever she went outside, she wore a surgical mask. The doctors said she had to wait until her poly count reached one thousand before she could move freely in crowds.

Three times a week, we drove for half an hour to Toronto Sick Kids for chemo and blood tests. We began to think numbers. We sat in the waiting room for the hour it took Ruby to go through the procedure. The doctors said she was in the group they called "average risk," which was someone her age with a white blood cell count of less than fifty thousand. My father, the optimist, said the best minds in the world were on top of this one. "She's being cured right now, as we speak," he'd say. Near the end of the session he'd leave and come back with a dozen Tim Horton's doughnuts for us to eat on the way home.

That winter, the house grew brittle with sickness. We were all cold. Ruby seemed to bruise at the mention of touch. The muscle that had once helped her fly was now gone. I saw in her eyes and the way she walked what the last few months had done to her, her back hooked like an old woman's to match her leathery hands. There was no bounce in her step. Her small body, once clean and powerful, was now frightening to look at. Wherever she went she left clumps of hair like balls of tangled transparent fishing line.

Quilts floated like magic blankets from my mother's sewing room. The fire blazed that winter, but somehow it couldn't warm the chill in our veins. Early spring storms came and went without my father's notice. Someone from the weather centre called to ask why we'd missed the tornado that had ripped up the bridge over the Ganaraska. When my father told them what was happening, no one called again.

In March, after three months of chemo, the maintenance therapy started. Just before Ruby's fourteenth birthday. I would turn eighteen that summer. Things began to level out. Most of the time Ruby was fine, except for the few days a month when she had to take her drugs. I began to read books on leukemia. It was called the children's cancer. I'd hoped an understanding of the disease would give us the upper hand. I left the books on my parents' bed before saying good night. I remembered my father's refrain from our storm-hunting days. *In scientia est salus*. In knowledge is safety. It had been proved wrong already. But it was the only thing I could do. Study and learn. My mother made blankets to keep Ruby from more harm. They covered her like a protecting skin. My father sat by her bed from the moment he returned from the shop until she fell asleep. My grandfather came on the train from Kingston as often as his failing health permitted. Among the books I signed out from the library were more studies of evolution.

I had already applied to the University of Chicago, where I hoped eventually to study advanced meteorological sciences under the eminent weather theorist, Professor Fujita. But by then I'd dropped severe weather as a hobby and turned to paleontology. I'd dissected Darwin's *The Origin of*

Species and considered every theory and counter-theory that it had spawned over the last one hundred and nineteen years, hoping that a pattern in our small lives would emerge against the backdrop of time.

And, for a time, it worked. Within a year, Ruby responded to her treatment. She was strong again. Her hair came back, a blonde curly mass. By mid-winter, it seemed she was on the road to complete remission. The count of leukemic blasts seemed to be bottoming out. Every week she went in for blood tests. The chemo was tapered off to nothing. I felt magnanimous. I wanted to celebrate. Into her second spring as an outpatient, I resolved to raise money for the March of Dimes. The same day I started working on a plan to break the world drown-proofing record, I went canvassing for sponsorships.

The River

A WEEK AFTER I recalled the history of Ruby's cancer, I went for the record in the public pool on the banks of Joshua Creek. The spring rain that ended up flooding our small town for the first time in over a hundred years started early that morning. The creek soon began to rise. I had a list of sponsors as long as my arm willing to pay good money if I walked away with a new record. I'd been in contact with Guinness. The time to beat had stood since 1967 at thirty-one hours, twenty-five minutes. All I had to do was to make it through to Sunday afternoon. I'd done the math. My pledges stood at just under eight thousand dollars, almost double if I beat the going record. But the flood was something I hadn't factored into the equation.

My parents came to wish me and my sister well that morning. Alicia was there, too, a friend from school, and half a dozen of my sponsors. Dressed in street clothes, they all stood on the cement deck under an overcast sky, looking down into the pool, shaking their heads in wonder and patting me and Ruby on the back. I was already in my bathing suit, a pair of red-tinted goggles hanging from an elastic around my neck. A warm breeze passed over us as my mother leaned forward and kissed me.

"Good luck," she said and kissed me again. "It's okay if you don't make it all the way through. We'll figure out something else if we have to."

But I would make it all the way through. It seemed natural that I should do this. My father worked for Oakville Sailing Ships, a company that built yachts down by the harbour. He hadn't sailed competitively for years; but now and then he took down a trophy from the fireplace mantel and told me its story, how a twenty-knot wind had come from the west on such-and-such day and practically lifted his two-man schooner right out of the water. There were always the stories of sailing the Dragon class in Rome. Anything that had to do with water and wind, he loved. On vacation, he sought out the sea. At a lake, he was the first to dip his toes in. At home, he was the last to get out of the pool before supper. I had taken after him, I thought. The drown proofing was just a natural extension of that. It was something carried in the veins.

But we knew Ruby carried something different in her veins. My parents worried about an anaemic reaction. Ruby had gained back the weight she'd lost and her hair had grown in again. She would be going to summer school to make up for time lost. Doctor Lee had told us physical exercise was an essential component of her therapy. My parents planned to come by every couple of hours to see how I was doing. Ruby was going to stay with me, act as a spotter along with three friends from school. This was part of her recuperation—becoming involved in life again after being apart for so long.

"Look out for your sister," my mother said into my ear, and hugged me. She knew this was too big for all of us to break off because of an overcast sky. I knew she wanted to release her into the world again. Maybe this was the final step to that. She pulled Ruby into her chest and held her there while my father and I shook hands.

"Don't forget—controlled breathing," he said. "And keep a clear head." He tapped his temple with a forefinger. "You're thinking for two," and raised his eyebrows in Ruby's direction.

An official from Oakville Parks and Recreation was there that morning, a large man in a blue tracksuit with a whistle around his neck. He was supposed to stay with me until he was relieved by another official, five in all over the space of the thirty-odd hours I was to be here. They were there to verify that I didn't touch the side or the bottom of the pool or cheat in any way.

I saw the first drop roll over the surface of the water as I stepped into the pool and swam out to the middle. It began slowly. Then when my parents and the sponsors all finally left, the real rain started. Big shimmering globes beating down on my head. The fat man retired to the slice of dry cement under the lip of the roof that overhung the entrance to the change rooms and read a newspaper for half an hour. From the middle of the pool I watched him polish the silver whistle against his sleeve. He looked up at the clouds, hesitated a moment.

Then folded the newspaper over his head and ran out to his car in the parking lot and drove away.

Joshua Creek snaked through Valley Park barely a hundred feet north of the pool. From the change-room entrance you could see it winding its way down through the valley until it disappeared behind a bend. Somewhere a mile or so downstream it drained its slow dark belly into Lake Ontario. From the water that morning I looked to the bridge that crossed over the creek just down from the pool to where half a dozen boys chased spawning suckers with sharpened hockey sticks. Crashing through the water under the bridge, they would stab one through the body, then throw the poor fish up onto the road to get squashed by a passing car.

Just Ruby and Alicia were left that morning after the man with the whistle drove away. Alicia was from my grade thirteen calculus class. She'd gone to the hospital with me a few times that winter to visit Ruby. Sitting side by side on the diving board, they caught raindrops on their tongues and sang to me, swaying back and forth against each other's shoulders. My sister walked around the deck sometimes, jumping up into a handstand, and let the rain drench her. Alicia read from *Wuthering Heights* and scooped out grass clippings and windblown leaves from the pool with the skimmer. Then Alicia would move the hand on the cardboard-and-plywood clock that Ruby had made so I'd always know where the countdown to the record stood. The clock sat to the right of the diving board. The wheel, where the numbers zero to thirty-one were pasted, spun under a bright-red stationary arrow at the top of the clock face. The final thirty-one was the record to beat. Ruby had placed an umbrella over the clock to keep the construction-paper numbers from washing away in the rain.

After about three hours, the boys began filtering up from the creek onto the bridge. One of them still had a live fish stuck to the end of his hockey stick, flapping sadly against the rain.

I held my breath and looked down through the water and counted the drowning worms as they nosed their way along the bottom. When I raised my head again Alicia was balancing the other umbrella on top of the silver railing of the diving board. The red fabric domed over their heads. I relaxed again and looked down. The tinted goggles turned the dew worms' dying motions a warm soft pink. All around me, the surface stuccoed with rain. When I floated face down, I felt its little fingers drumming hard against my back. I looked up and caught my breath. "Think this'll last?" It sounded like I was talking about Ruby's leukemia. "The rain," I said, correcting myself.

It'll clear for sure. That's what we'd all said the day we discovered she was sick, as if it was a question of filtering skunky water from a swimming pool. She sat under the beach umbrella with her knees tucked into her chest. My eyes were the same level as her feet. Five years without recurrence was considered complete remission. She'd been in remission under a year. But the doctors said her progress was remarkable. She was blessed. She seemed back to her old self. I watched her as she jumped up into another handstand under the overhang by the change rooms. Upside down, facing me, she held herself in position and smiled. Then she came back down and stretched her arms behind her and puffed out her chest like she'd done at the qualifying meet in Toronto.

The trees around the pool drooped under the weight of rain, leaves turning a richer, darker spring green, the constant splashing playing on the surface of the water. A little boy, already soaked, appeared at the fence then and hooked his fingers into the mesh. For a time before he spoke, he watched the three of us intently.

"Why are you in there?" he said.

Months before, when Ruby had asked me why I wasn't

interested in breaking a swimming record, I told her that the Dead Man's Float was a thinking man's gig. We were sitting in the beanbag chair when I told her about my plans. I got up and turned off the TV. It was about endurance and hope, I said, not speed, and hope was something we'd learned while she was going through her treatment. There was all that time in the water to wonder about things while you waited for someone to rescue you, and there was no shortage of things to hope for in life. Especially now, after what she'd been through the last year and a half.

"Only controlled proofing counts," I'd said. "Harbour patrol pulling in a guy somewhere in the middle of the lake after three days is different. Verification is crucial." I asked her if she wanted to be one of my spotters. "It's for a good cause."

"What's it for?" she said.

"So you won't get sick anymore."

Ruby helped me train that spring. Between the time I spent at the pool and going to class I looked for sponsors. I asked everyone at school for a dollar an hour, students and teachers. Most of them knew Ruby. By then they'd heard she'd been in hospital. My history teacher put herself down for five dollars an hour with the promise to double her pledge if I broke the record. Her son had died in a car accident two years before. After I'd asked just about everyone at school, I started knocking on doors around the neighbourhood and went to the two other Oakville high schools.

After more than two months of organizing and pleading and scrounging, the Valley Park Public Outdoor Pool was the only pool in town willing to go along with my plan. Everyone else talked about liability. We couldn't use our pool at home because there was some concern about neutrality. Plus, we'd never opened it before July. So I convinced the Valley Park people to throw open their doors one weekend ahead of schedule. At first they were reluctant. But my principal got involved and then someone told the March of Dimes that I wanted to raise some money for them and the Valley Park pool was shamed into opening early, as well as providing the services of the fat man with the whistle who left after only two hours.

After the little boy had asked that question, Why was I in here? he lingered by the fence for a time, kicking idly at the muddy ground like he was waiting for me to invite him in. I imagined myself as he saw me. It was a little crazy, I knew, bobbing up and down like this in the rain. Floating like a cadaver. I looked over to Ruby skimming the surface of the water and thought about what she'd been through. I took a deep breath and hung my head between my shoulders. Out of the corner of my eye I saw the skimmer break the surface of the water; my sister's fractured reflection standing up on the deck, peened by falling rain. The legs looked bent and crooked. I turned my head down to the bottom and tried to remember the time before spinal taps and chemo, before tufts of blonde hair had begun gathering on Ruby's pillow every morning. When I came back up, the boys who'd been killing suckers were standing at the fence, sharpened hockey sticks tossed over their shoulders like rifles. One of them still had a fish on the end of his stick but it wasn't wiggling anymore. The little boy was gone. They just stood there watching, silently punching each other in the shoulders.

The rain fell all morning. After four hours it started to bother me. I started to notice it. When I pulled my face out of the water to breathe, it tickled my face as it dripped between my eyes and rolled off my nose. But it wasn't affecting what I was doing. A warm rain, cooler than the pool, but warm enough. Alicia and Ruby had changed and were sitting, warm and dry, under the overhang where the official had read his newspaper before he left.

At hour five, when I saw my father appear at the fence, I

thought he'd come to get me. He held a large green garbage bag in his right hand. Ruby came out from under the soffit carrying an umbrella. I edged over to the side of the pool.

"Opa's doctor called. His lungs have flooded. Catch." He tossed the bag over the fence to Ruby. "Some things your mother threw together. Warm clothes." He put his hands in the mesh. "We've got to go to Kingston." Then he stopped, considering. "Where's Mr. Kowalchuk?" He meant the official.

"Bathroom," Ruby said before I could answer.

"Here's the number of the hospital in Kingston. Room 504." He passed a piece of paper through the fence, then touched Ruby's face with an extended finger. "Stay out of the rain, sweetie."

Then he called out to me, "Everything okay?" I could see he was worried about his dad. My grandfather was alone in Kingston, the old sailor, fading now. I imagined my father standing by his sickbed, the old hand in his, fragile, thin as his breathing. My father grinned at me sadly when I gave him the thumbs up, then disappeared around the side of the building.

At suppertime, after I drank a couple of bottles of fruit juice and ate some granola bars and trail mix, the night shift came by to relieve Alicia and Ruby. Mike and Susan brought a guitar and a twelve-pack of Carlsberg. They carried a picnic table from around the side of the building and sat under the umbrella they'd hooked up to it, the two of them, drinking and playing and flicking beer caps at me.

"Get outta here, you guys," I said, shielding my head with an outstretched hand. "Stop it. Play 'Like a Hurricane.' " The flood lamps were on now, casting a dome of light over the pool. After he drank his first beer, Mike started playing. I watched the rain come down in sheets against the glow of light. I'd been trying to conserve energy the whole time. By now I could tell for what. I was starting to feel it. I was just barely past the halfway mark. The water level of the pool had risen flush with the deck. As he tapped his foot along to the music, small splashes rolled towards me out to the centre of the pool. When he finished singing I asked Susan to go into the pool house and turn up the heater a touch. The water was slowly chilling.

For each beer they drank, I finished a bottle of orange juice. At midnight, Alicia and Ruby came back from the house. The rain was still coming down. I thought they'd come to wish me luck for the night. But they didn't seem to be in any hurry.

"For as long as it takes," Alicia said, holding the umbrella between them.

"But Susan and Mike're here," I said. "You can't stay up all night."

"I called Mom and Dad. Opa's okay. But they're keeping him in the hospital overnight. I told them I was going to bed. They'll be home tomorrow."

Ruby climbed up onto the picnic table with Alicia then and sat snugly under the big umbrella. Mike strummed again. I hovered all the while, bobbing up and down in the water a few feet from the edge.

Ruby got up and walked into the change room and came back out a minute later in her bathing suit. She stood beside the pool for a second, her hand out to the falling rain. She was drenched before she touched the water.

"You're not allowed to come in."

"You heard the doctors," she said. "Exercise. Anyway, it's chlorinated."

Water rolled over the deck when she jumped in. She came back to the surface and went under for a second and came back up at an angle to pull the hair away from her eyes, then swam out to meet me. "No biggy. See," she said. "I'm still alive."

Together we floated like the dead bobbing on a shipwrecked sea. Music from Mike's guitar echoed down through the water. Ruby blurred in the light from above, arms out-stretched. We peered for the bottom. After she ran out of breath she brought her head back up.

"It's like floating in space," she said, panting.

She dipped her head under again and her feet shot up into the air and immediately slid through a slit in the water. I held my breath and looked down. She kept herself against the bottom, arms moving sideways to help her lie flat on her back. She smiled up at me, floating above her in the full face of the cratering surface. Then she pushed back up for air.

Just then a muted roar came up out of the darkness from the gully to the left above the bridge where the boys had been killing fish. Mike stopped playing.

"Listen," he said. "You can hear the river now." He flicked a beer cap at me. "Not a good sign."

Empty bottles were piling up over the deck. The cardboard beer case was soaked through, swollen like a sponge. I wondered if the drains built into the deck could absorb the water spilling over the sides of the pool.

"Check this out," he said. He touched one of the empty beer bottles on the deck with his foot. It didn't clank against the cement. It bobbed, turning slightly, and floated a few feet before it got stuck on something. "The whole park must be under a foot of water."

"I think it's time you all got outta here," I said. The clock showed sixteen hours proofed. "Only halfway to go now." It was just past midnight.

"We're not leaving you here," Susan said.

"We couldn't get wetter than we already are," Ruby said, floating off my right elbow.

"Isn't it time you got out?" I said.

"Look. It's slowing down," Alicia said.

The surface of the pool extended beyond the deck and the fence. But it wasn't bubbling with rain as it had earlier. It was still raining, but not like before.

For the past hour I'd been feeling a slight current pulling me from the centre of the pool in the direction the beer bottles had been swept. I guessed Ruby was still strong enough not to notice it. Down at the bottom, the water was as quiet as it had been from the start. But the surface was moving towards Lake Ontario. I felt it as clearly as a wind moving over my face. In the light cast out by the flood lamps over the change-room entrances, water was curling around the cinder-block corners of the building, the stems of crabgrass vibrating lightly under the pressure of the swollen river.

"It's for a good cause," Susan said. "I'm willing to stick it out." We all looked at Ruby.

She hung there beside me on the flooding surface like a drowning tree, like a dead-head on a sleeping lake.

When the sun rose that morning I saw a different landscape than the one I remembered from the day before. The rain had stopped. But it was all water and tree branches now. There was no grass, no pavement or roads or gravel walkways. The houses and cars up on the embankment were safe. But the single road that cut down from the embankment and passed over the bridge was covered. It was all under water. The tops of swing sets and monkey bars stood above the current, catching debris as it floated by. Silently, I'd watched the water level of the pool rise all night. Ruby had gotten out somewhere around one o'clock and gone inside the change room with Alicia and Susan to get some sleep. Mike had stayed to keep me company. I'd watched the river rise steadily against the cinder blocks of the change house until there was no swaying crabgrass left to be seen. Over the course of the night I'd been pulled down close to the south end of the pool, pulled slowly in the direction of the run-off. For hours now I'd been careful to pull back against the current. Just before light broke I'd heard a low grinding, then a snap. When the sun rose I saw the half-submerged skeletons of the merry-go-round and playground swings on the other side of the fence. That's when I noticed where the snap had come from. The fence around the perimeter of the pool looked lower than I remembered it. Over the night the flood had deposited bundles of newspaper and sopping leaves and tree branches on it and bent it over a few feet in the direction of the flow. The building that housed the change rooms had acted as a breakwater for me, had slowed the current around me like a heavy rock in a stream. I knew that was the only reason I was still here.

At seven that morning Mike passed me a granola bar and some juice. He joined me for breakfast and looked out over the park. "This is incredible," he said. "The whole valley's under. I must have dozed. You okay?"

I released the juice bottle in the water and watched it float out of the pool, over the deck and through the broken section of fence. It rode the current like a toy boat and met up with more junk: bundles of newspaper, an old chair, plastic bags, branches, and a dead seagull. I saw Ruby's clock caught against a tree a hundred yards downstream, just before the bend in the river. It was too far away to make out what time it was set at.

"Without the change house, I'd be gone."

"I'm sorry for dozing," he said, shaking his head.

"Just let me finish what I started, that's all."

Junk drifted past on the current just outside what was left of the fence. Mike waded over the deck and woke up the girls. They walked out in water up to their knees, speechless, rubbing their eyes. They climbed onto the picnic table. After breakfast Ruby went back into the change room, came out again in her bathing suit, and jumped in with me.

"How are you doing?" she said, swimming up close.

I told her I was okay. She swam to the side and paddled back holding some trail mix above the water.

"Think it'll count after this?" I said. "The record, I mean."

"Of course."

"No one other than us is here." Our feet and hands were spreading in calm water-pushing circles below us. "There's no neutral bodies."

"They'll believe us. Four witnesses."

"But we're a bunch of kids," I said. There was a pause.

She was considering that when Mike yelled some obscenity about his guitar floating away.

"The clock, too," Susan said, pointing to where I'd seen it wedged up against the oak. I let another bottle go and Ruby and I watched it spin in the current and leave through the hole in the fence. I pushed back against the current again, up closer to the change house. Ruby came up behind me. "Has it been pulling you like this all night?"

"It's getting stronger," I said. I was breathing short breaths. "Time check."

"Seven-thirty-five," Susan called out. "That's about six more hours to tie. Anything after that's gravy."

As the dimmed sun rose I saw the colour of the pool had changed. The water was brown now, not the perfect chlorinated blue of yesterday. I could still see the bottom, but it was murky. Colder, too.

"Are you up to it?" Ruby said. We were drifting faster now. I could feel the water pulling us. On the deck, the water was almost as high as the picnic-table seats. Mike brought out three chairs from the men's change room and stacked them against the eaves-trough spout that ran up the side of the building. First he climbed up onto the roof. Then he lay on his stomach and reached his arm down and helped Susan up, then Alicia.

"Don't think we're abandoning you," he called down. "Lifeguards have to have a superior vantage point."

"Ruby, you should get up there, too," I said.

But she just lifted her arms above her head and went under. For the first time I followed her all the way down, still careful not to touch bottom. I didn't want to disqualify myself. I hovered down there, inches from two bent beer caps and a knot of drowned worms, cupping upwards to keep myself under. Ruby arched and tilted back her head and rolled upside down. She did a one-arm handstand. I clapped in slow underwater motions, my cheeks puffed. Then I felt myself bump against the bottom, pushed and dragged. There was a sudden shift. Ruby lost her balance and went over. We looked at each other as we kicked for the surface but the pool had suddenly deepened. The distance to air had lengthened in an instant. We were deeper than we'd been hardly seconds before, as if a great sluice had been opened at the top of the valley. We grabbed each other's hands and fought upwards, spinning and twisting. I felt my back scrape against cement and we were carried out over the broken fence, out beyond the perimeter of the pool, hanging together as we were pulled into the broad sweep of the river until we came up gasping and clutching. "Keep holding," I said. My mouth was grainy with river water. In a moment the current had driven us out to the middle of the flooded park. I felt for the bottom but there was nothing. Houses sat up on higher land, unaffected by the flood. There wasn't anything we could swim for, just a Javex bottle and small planks of wood and bundles of garbage.

When we turned the bend in the river we saw the time clock wedged against a tall oak. The construction-paper numbers were washed away now. The red arrow indicated nothing, like a finger pointing in the dark. When we reached the oak we joined hands and pulled ourselves up onto the clock. It would offer some support, I thought. But once we'd partly dragged ourselves up onto the plywood, the clock came free from the oak and we began moving with the river again, swirling in small, gentle circles. Up on the embankment, houses drifted past like remote, unreachable islands. After the bend where Rebecca Street ran parallel to the river, the water grew calmer still, the floodplain broadened. Street signs looked down through the maples into the valley. At this rate we'd be at the harbour in a few minutes. I knew that we weren't going to drown. But I was worried about Ruby. I imagined my mother when she found out about this, fearful that this flood would send her daughter back to another series of spinal taps and intensive chemo.

On a Tuesday morning we buried my grandfather in a Kingston cemetery. For a time, his health had seemed to improve. But the sudden second build-up of fluids in his lungs came and he died before anyone could help him. Now, except for us and his sister, my father was alone. All his people were gone.

We buried him beside my grandmother. My aunt was there that day, up from California, awkward on her crutches as she stood above the grave. The pastor spoke and then we each followed behind my father and dipped a silver spoon into a small bucket and sprinkled my grandfather's coffin with earth. After my turn I stood beside my father.

Marian took Ruby by the arm and pulled a strand of hair away from her face. My mother took Ruby by the shoulder, steadying her. She let the earth slip and fall into the hole. I lowered my head. The hair on the back of my neck pricked up as the falling earth spilled over the belly of the coffin like a slowly filling hourglass. I heard the clicking of my aunt's leg braces as she turned from the hole and started across the lawn.

Endings

RUBY RETURNED TO school that fall, and in October she was back at the gym. I was working at my father's shop now, saving money for the following year, when I would be leaving for Chicago. It was a quiet winter after my grandfather's passing. But by December Ruby was back on a modest training program. She was talking about Moscow again. Our family began to breathe freely. There was no reason she couldn't go. She had more than two years before they'd be choosing the next Olympic team. Boris talked to my parents about it, and to the doctors at Sick Kids. He wanted to know how hard he could push her. My mother bit her lip and frowned; the doctors assured her that it was best for a recovering patient to get back into the routine of his or her normal life. Physical exercise would just help the process along. Her red blood cell count was normal; there was little or no fear of anaemic reactions.

There were small gym meets that winter. Ruby watched from the bleachers. She still wasn't a hundred per cent. Her friends spun through the air over her head, twisting. She wasn't jealous. It made her work harder. Before she could take to the uneven bars, she remapped her routines over and over in her mind, flew higher than she'd ever flown before. "I'm refuelling," she'd say. Clouds raced through her head.

Her spirit soared in anticipation of her body. In June she took to the air again after almost two years of treatment and recovery. My parents and I sat at the picnic table before supper and watched her perform a tentative flip or a handstand, then lower herself into the splits, beaming up at us as if she was performing these moves for the very first time.

"Careful," my mother would say, more out of habit than fear.

"Look, Boobs," I said when she finally sat down at the picnic table. "Do either of us have any excuse now?"

"*Nyet*," she said, leaning into my father's chest. We were back on track after some minor evolutionary setbacks. Our mother began making clothes again after a year and a half of blankets. There hadn't been any problems with my father's sailboats since the disappearance off St. Lucia more than two years before. Our summer hummed with the sound of a Laser cutting through perfect wind and water, the jib finely tuned to the world.

That summer she competed for the first time in two and a half years. In the Ontario championships, Ruby took gold in floor and vault and pulled in the bronze for total points. We were all there to watch. Even my mother started thinking about a trip to Moscow. The doctors at Sick Kids predicted a complete remission. I'd be leaving for the University of Chicago in a month.

In July, a week after the meet, Ruby developed a sore throat. For two days we watched the cough. They took her to

Toronto for her weekly tests. I saw them off that morning, then got into my bathing suit and dove into the pool. After a hundred laps I stopped in the middle of the deep end, filled my lungs and relaxed my arms. I looked down through the water. I thought about what it would be like to be dead, maybe something like this, floating just above and below the surface of things. Being in more than one place at a time. I watched my feet hanging below me, motionless as water-logged sticks, as if they were no longer a part of me. I hadn't broken the record, but I'd raised over three thousand dollars. I wiggled a toe and saw it move. The thinking man's game, I thought. Floating between life and death.

Two hours later I heard the car pull into the driveway. I was warming down now doing slow lengths of the pool. Ruby came around back and kicked off her sneakers and sat on the grass. She was singing a Bee Gees song. Then she went upstairs to get into her bathing suit.

My mother and father came out into the backyard and sat down on the deck. My father leaned over and touched the water with his finger. "Warm," he said, considering something. "Peter. She's out of remission."

"But they said they got all the blasts."

"There's been a relapse. They said it takes only a few

leukemic cells to take over the whole body again. Her red cell count's taken a nosedive. She's having an anaemic reaction. That explains the cough. Dr. Lee says there's an operation she has to have if they can get her into remission again. It's a transplant. It's the last option. He needs to take something out of your hip and give it to Ruby."

I rested my chin in my hands on the wooden deck, the noon sun warming my shoulders. I'd read a dozen books on leukemia by now. I knew what was going to be asked of me. I kicked my feet behind me and raised my body parallel to the surface.

"That's where the blood's made," my mother said. "It's called bone marrow." She touched my arm. "They kill all of the bone marrow cells in Ruby, and give her some of your healthy cells. Not just the leukemic ones. They destroy everything. It's best if it's from a brother or a sister. That's the best chance she's got. Then she starts producing her own. But they have to test your blood to see if you're compatible. If you are, you could do it."

The screen door slid open then and Ruby walked onto the patio in her bathing suit. She didn't look sick to me. She looked tanned and healthy. She still didn't know about the relapse. I climbed out of the pool.

"Ruby, it's back," my mother said when she came up to the

three of us. She understood, just from that, and sat down at the edge of the pool, her feet hanging motionless in the water, and cried.

The next morning she was back at the hospital and on chemo again, hooked up to the IV, her head sideways on the pillow, turned towards the sky on the other side of the window. There was another spinal tap that night. When they pulled out the big butterfly needle, a nurse called me into the next room for my blood sample.

Within a week they determined we had nearly identical HLA antigens. There was a match.

Then, the radiotherapy. We watched her on the video monitor, her head strapped down to the flat surface to prevent any movement. Beside us in the booth, the technician gave Ruby some last-minute instructions over the microphone. "Remember, honey. Absolutely still, okay?" The hum of heavy, slow-moving machines. On the lead-covered door a sign read CAUTION—HIGH RADIATION AREA. The woman looked at me and mouthed, *All right.*

I brought my face close to the microphone and began to read.

" 'One day in 1802, a college student named Pliny Moody,

while plowing his father's field in South Hadley, Massachusetts, turned up a sandstone slab bearing the imprint of a large three-toed foot. It looked like the footprint of a giant turkey or raven.' " I looked up at the screen and said, "You copy? Over." I waited.

Over the speaker we heard her thin, metallic voice. "I copy."

" 'Those who saw this wonder decided, in a moment of pious fancy, that the print must have been made by the raven that Noah had released from the arc to search for dry land.' "

"Only a few minutes, honey," my father said, his face pressed against mine. They'd said there was no pain involved. She was laced to the earth like a helpless Gulliver. When the hum of the machines died, the technician went into the chamber and turned Ruby over. She came back out and started the radiation again.

" 'Other tracks of Noah's raven were found over the years, always in the Triassic sandstone that would become the source of the "brownstone" favoured in the construction of Manhattan townhouses.' "

"Would you like to see that some day, Ruby?" my mother asked into the microphone. "Go to America to see dinosaur fossils in the houses there?"

"I want it to stop," she said weakly. "Over."

Three weeks of this, roped to the hard board in the radiation room. She lost weight rapidly. Her hair fell out again. She was back to where she started. Every day, radiotherapy. I wondered if she carried around the poison rays once they'd turned off the machine. A fire cooking inside her body.

"All this is going somewhere," I told her. "Archaeopteryx didn't know he was turning into a bird when it was happening." There were dark circles under her eyes. Her head looked too big for her body. I didn't know if she understood what I wanted her to understand.

"What a funny thing I'll turn out to be," she said. "This mix, you and me."

Already into September, a week before the transplant was set to go, I called the dean of sciences at the University of Chicago to explain what was happening to my family. In the letter she returned to me a week later granting a deferral, she said the university would be pleased to have a student as dedicated to family as I seemed to be. She enclosed a *Scientific American* article that touted miraculous advances in leukemia research and treatment. She ended the letter, *Godspeed*.

Before the operation, I dreamt Ruby and I flew. She carried me on her back. Bathed in sunlight, Lake Ontario opened before us. We broke the surface and went under. As we went deeper and deeper I blew oxygen into my sister's mouth. We found a treasure chest at the edge of an underwater mountain full of syringes and leukemic blasts. We loaded the needles and squeezed their milky substance into the pale water and watched the thinned cancerous blood dissipate through streaked sunlight descended from the surface.

The nurses encouraged me to walk a few hours after I came out of the anaesthetic. Still in my pyjamas, I rode the elevator and limped down the hall to Ruby's room. By the time I got there, she'd already received the first bag of marrow they'd taken from me. It hung on a rack beside the bed, like an IV, but the tube was hooked up directly below her collarbone. The doctor said everything looked good so far. She felt feverish; her head pounded. I felt nauseated. All the side effects we'd been warned about. But the pain in my bones began to subside. It felt like I was carrying gravel in my hips. They did tests before they hooked up a second, paler bag. We waited there with her for the two hours it took to complete the transplant, watching the bag's yellow-pink contents move along the tube and disappear into Ruby's chest, the afternoon sun streaming through the open window. She was kept in isolation to minimize the risk of infection.

After a month, the rejection began. Her body turned red with blotches. It was the mixing of our blood, I thought. Her skin turned scaly. It had nothing to do with the HLA antigens. We'd evolved in different directions. What I'd given was killing her. Every day, after he finished work, my father drove me to Toronto. My mother was always there, waiting. Ruby would ask me to scratch her back when our parents went out to the hallway to consult with Doctor Lee. I'd slide my hand under her shoulder blades and lightly run my fingers up and down her spine. I felt the drying skin come off in my hand. "Softer," she'd say, and me barely touching her. The tests confirmed it. They called it Graft Versus Host Disease. Her skin burned; the diarrhea threatened to drain all the liquids from her body. I was the graft. It was me doing this to her. It was my blood that was killing her.

Skeletal now, her shoulder blades emerged from her body like great wings. Small like a bird, and bird-like, her mind jumped suddenly from post to wire. Her breaths were short. *Yes, scratch there*, she'd say. And then appearing on a branch. *Cold like an icicle! Remember how I told you it was?* And of a sudden, screeching, *I want to go home. Over!* The final attempts to rise. *Booby*, I'd say, taking the hand to my face.

Helpless that last week, we watched as her thoughts soared.

Perched on black-iron weathervanes, surveying, then breaking free in a desperate flutter of wing and feather. When open, her eyes glowed with an understanding gathered from dizzying heights. *How sad, the end of the Triassic,* clawing against air; her voice thin now as her wrists. *Countdown to Moscow.* For days, her body receding along a parade of nurses and doctors. Always my mother or father staying behind while I went home with the other to rest.

"Sweetheart?" my father said that last morning, sinking to his knees. Her clawed hands scratched against air as they might have done her first day in hospital fourteen years before. Her small body writhed in its attempt to fly. A desperate fluttering, the straining effort to leave the world beneath her, one last time. Then the quiet stillness, Ruby somewhere distant as my mother, all month fighting tears, hoping for her child's quick death. All of us. We knew what each was thinking. Eagerly now, we waited for the silence to come and wrap his dark glove over her heart. Without words my mother kneeled beside my father as my sister rose, her life spiralling upwards like windfall over dark water.

V

From the stands Rudolph watched the man dig the hole into the dirt track with the hand trowel to the correct size of his left shoe. He watched him as he measured the distance for the second hole along the length of his thigh. He marked a second spot in the dirt, verified its accuracy by placing his forward foot into the new hole and finding where his right foot fell comfortably. He ground his toe into the dirt, then trowelled out the hole into the shape of his right shoe. The runner righted himself and straightened his back. He put down the tool and crouched and set both feet into the holes, first the left, then the right. His knee came up against his chest when he sank into starting position. He bobbed, putting pressure on the balls of his feet, testing to see if the dirt would hold. He removed his feet and made adjustments. The other runners, three on his left, one on his right, were ready now. They were standing, shaking out their legs and slapping their thighs. Rudolph admired the man's concentration. He would not be rushed. Finally he stood and tossed the trowel onto the grassy infield where a chubby man in a white suit scurried and bent to collect it. The tool disappeared into the pail he carried under his right arm. The runner shook out his legs and looked up at the sky.

"*Auf die Plätze,*" the starter called. The five men took their mark and waited, thighs wet and blood-filled, feet tight in the dirt starting blocks. Rudolph readied his camera. Overhead, the shadow of the *Hindenburg* nosed out the sun. Its straining motors buzzed through the silence like insects. Its shadow fed along the contours of muscle.

"*Fertig.*"

The pistol shot rang out. Immediately followed by another. Rudolph lifted his finger from the button and exhaled. The airship passed overhead as the men walked back to their starting positions, averting their eyes from one another.

SEVERE WEATHER

IT MAY HAVE been the mystery of wind then, the spinning of my sister's mobile above her crib, which eventually led me to the storms. The wind that made those paper-napkin snowflakes dance. I watched summer air breathe under the billowing curtains of her nursery window. Through the slats of her crib I watched the flickerings of understanding move across her face like a sheet of rain over water. Her hands outstretched, upwards. Ignoring me in her concentration.

The year I turned six, two years after we brought my sister home from hospital, my father drove me through the heart of my first tornado.

He was a storm hunter in those days, also drawn to wind. Through the Ontario Weather Centre he'd find out about a storm moving across-province and drive headlong into it at eighty miles an hour with nothing more than a thermos of black coffee and a couple of ham and cheese sandwiches sitting beside him on the passenger seat. Sometimes he'd leave the house at three in the morning to chase one down. He loved all types of severe weather: waterspouts, funnel clouds, flooding downpours, hailstorms, dust devils, and heat lightning. But above all he loved tornadoes.

Everyone at the Ontario Weather Centre knew my father in those days. He used to phone in seven days a week looking for reports of significant weather gathering on the horizon or blowing in from the lakes, then race out of the house like a man late for his own wedding. But he understood storms better than anyone. Sometimes even better than the men at the Centre. He was only an amateur storm watcher, but they often used his reports. They'd ask his opinion concerning certain storms: what one was doing, where it was headed. In the strange cabal of significant weather watchers, my father was quickly making a name for himself. And I wasn't far behind.

My mother, on the other hand, never cared for storms. By then she had taken to wearing her long red hair done up in a bun, as if battened down tightly against unexpected winds. She worked part-time at the Centennial Public Library, organizing something she called "The Bear Pit." With the help of government subsidies, she brought in speakers from around the province in an effort to enlighten our small community. Historians and poets, jugglers, race-car drivers. She decided who came, and each speaker was paid a stipend for his or her trouble. My father, who would have been an obvious choice, who could have marvelled the uninitiated with tales of storm hunting, never took the lectern. My mother never asked him; and he never volunteered. I knew hunting storms was a sore spot between them, first because it was a dangerous and crazy thing to be involved in, and later, after Ruby died, because severe weather became as threatening to their marriage as an exotic woman who came crashing through town, staying just long enough to get my father to do something rash or unpredictable.

"This man lived with cannibals in New Guinea for twenty-five years," my mother would say at the supper table. Or "So-and-so climbed to the top of Mount Everest," and she'd send a sidelong glance over to my father, the drifting smile that moved over her face when she believed she had something that would finally capture my interest. "The incredible thing is he's only got *one arm*. Can you imagine the kind of man it takes to do something like that!" My father, though, tall and forward-leaning, would sit at the kitchen table impassively, unimpressed, rolling his peas around on his plate with his fork and plotting in his head the course of the nearest squall line or reviewing statistics from *The Weekly Review of Canadian Climate and Water.*

My mother brought me along to many of the Bear Pit sessions. I listened to the stories of a man who'd rolled across the country in a wheelchair; a woman who kept more than two hundred snakes in her basement; the life story of a pair of Siamese twins, now separated. But since the age of ten, storms were my passion. I knew the difference between bead lightning and ball lightning, and that the scientific community was split on whether the latter actually existed. By the time I was thirteen I knew more about storms than any science teacher at school. I won first prize for my grade nine science fair project when I produced a contained tornado by joining two Coke bottles at the neck with a snipped balloon end, one holding ten ounces of water. The clincher was when I rated the strength of my homemade storm on a miniaturized Fujita F-scale, calculating the strength of my whirlwind and the damage in real dollars that an equivalent full-scale tornado would bring to our small town. I knew that a tornado was called a "funnel cloud" until it came to earth, and that Ontario's hail season had begun on schedule that same year when hailstones were reported at Cootes Paradise on the fourteenth of March and would probably last upwards of a hundred and seventy days, well into September. I knew during our last severe weather season we'd had twenty-nine tornadoes across the province, concentrated into fourteen storm days. During a severe weather season that lasted some forty-five days, fourteen tornado days made for about a thirty per cent season. My father and I had witnessed seven.

Whatever points I gained in science class when I was a kid, my father and I lost at home with my mother. Although she insisted on taking me to her Bear Pit sessions all the way up to grade twelve, deep down inside I think she realized whose footsteps I would follow in since the day my father took me to see that first tornado.

"We've got sightings of funnels out near Tillsonburg," he said, writing something in the pad of paper he always kept with him. Ruby was upstairs having a nap under that snowstorm mobile. He'd just gotten off the phone with the weather centre. It had been tracking a thunderstorm for the last few hours. I remember looking out the window at the still trees across the street, then at my mother. She was standing at the sink, scraping leftovers into a plastic Tupperware dish. My father closed the notepad and slid his pencil behind his right ear. "If we're lucky, it'll turn into something serious and suck up a cow or two," he said and winked at me. My mother turned around and glared at him icily.

As we drove west to Tillsonburg, my father told me what I could expect from a storm like the one we were heading into. He said if the funnel decided to touch down it would only be a baby tornado. "Barely an F-0," he said. I didn't understand this new language. As he spoke his eyes roamed the horizon, hoping, I knew, for airborne material. Every fifteen minutes he radioed into the weather centre with an update.

"We might not see anything today," he said to me as he drove. "I should warn you. But they've got funnel sightings coming into the centre. That's a good sign, at least. Tornadoes are finicky things." It seemed to me that he was trying to be upbeat.

Between reports over the CB I learned how less than one per cent of thunderstorms manifest themselves as tornadoes, how all conditions have to be just right for one to form. I learned that the world-renowned meteorologist, Professor T. Theodore Fujita, had just developed an ingenious system which helped predict a tornado's potential destructiveness based on its wind speed. Backtracking, my father explained the Fujita system to me thoroughly, interrupting himself now and then to ask if I had any questions. "No," I said, slowly pouring him some black coffee from the thermos, trying to remember all the things he'd just told me. A gust of wind bumped the car ever so slightly, as if to lend weight and credibility to my father's understanding of tornadoes, his explanation of the heavens, and a hot black ribbon of coffee jumped into my lap from the spout.

"What you can explain can't hurt you," he said as I handed him the coffee, the stain spreading across my thigh. "There's nothing to be afraid of from a tornado if you know what you're dealing with. *In scientia est salus.*" He stopped talking and blew over his coffee. "I guess you know your mom doesn't approve of me bringing you out here."

"Is she mad at us?"

"No, she's not. But she's a girl," he said, "and girls don't understand the fun stuff like storms."

The afternoon turned black around four o'clock and two miles east of Delhi we pulled over to the side of the road and let the centre of a baby F-0 tornado pass over us.

"Roll down your window," my father said excitedly. Newspapers and plastic bags whirled frantically around the car. A pick-up truck and two other cars stopped on the side of the road, more storm hunters like my father. I rolled down the window and a gust of wind reached in and whipped up my hair. Sand and grit blew over my face. "Stick out your hand," he said. He had his window rolled down the same as mine. "You're touching it, Peter!" he shouted. "You're shaking hands with a tornado!"

After the tornado dissipated we got out of the car and talked to the other storm watchers. I didn't understand much of what they said. My knowledge of storms was still limited to what my father had told me on our way here. I stood beside him, holding his hand while they compared notes. He knew them from other sightings. They all knew each other's names. My father offered around his coffee and sandwiches, and an old lady from Bond Head cut a slice of chocolate cake for me, which I ate sitting on the hood of our car. On our way home my father asked me again if I had any questions about what we'd seen. Outside of Cambridge he pulled into a Dairy Queen and bought us each an ice cream cone.

"We saw a storm," I said to Ruby when we got home. She was watching a sparrow hop about in the grass on the front lawn. There was conspiracy in my voice. A secret that we would share. I whispered in her ear. "I shook hands with the tornado. This hand." I showed her. I wanted to let her know that I understood why her mobile fascinated her so. She looked at me and smiled.

But my family changed with Ruby's death. Winds churned in ways I'd never known. My mother tried to look forward. She was determined that her sorrow wouldn't interfere with whatever future we had left. I saw her trying. I knew she was looking inside herself. But my first summer back from the University of Chicago I saw my father's grief had nowhere to go but out into that strange world of storms and I learned who my mother was finally, where she'd been all those years.

My father and I were going to mark our thirteenth storm season together by shooting for a thirty per cent view rate, which meant roughly ten individual tornadoes, a third of what the province could expect to experience in one season. During our best season we'd managed barely twenty per cent, mostly F-0s and F-1s. We'd have to make it to one in three tornadoes of the expected thirty or so, not including waterspouts, dust devils, and funnel clouds. We were aiming high, but I believed I was ready for it. I was at the head of my class. The University of Chicago offered one of the most respected meteorology graduate programs on the continent. I'd taken to sitting in on Fujita's lectures every Friday afternoon in the temple-like silence of the Hinds Building. I already had a job lined up for next summer at the Pikes Peak synoptic weather station in Colorado, 14,110 feet above sea level. I'd gotten it through my first-year physics professor, whose brother headed the National Meteorological Center in Camp Springs, Maryland. Come next June, I'd have a bird's-eye view of the entire northwestern quarter of the continent. On any given morning, I'd be one of the first on the planet to taste whatever new weather system the heavens cared to bring, to rake my fingers through a particular cloud formation, as unique and evanescent as any palm print, to marvel at its particular wash of pink-and-grey light. I believed I could do anything.

I was working at the head office of the Ministry of the Environment in downtown Toronto that summer, compiling data for a study on the effects severe weather had on the farming industry in southwestern Ontario. On a Tuesday afternoon my father called the office from his shop. Barb, my supervisor, handed me the phone.

"Peter," he said. "We've got a serious squall line moving in from the southwest. I think it's time the both of us suddenly develop a headache. Meet you out front. I'm leaving now."

"All right. Thank you," I said, and handed the phone back to Barb. I waited for a few minutes, put my forehead in my hands, leaned over my desk, and then started moaning. I asked if anyone around the office had a bottle of aspirin. A minute later, I keeled over. "A dizzy spell. That's all," I said as Barb rose from her desk. I waved her away. "Nothing to worry about," I insisted.

"We'll see about that," she said. "Call in tomorrow to let us know how you're feeling." She guided me through the door and down the corridor. For good measure I bumped off a wall as I weaved my way down the hall to the elevators. I leaned my head against the door in case she was still watching me until the bell chimed and I slipped in and the doors closed behind me. Twenty minutes later my father and I were on the 400 due north, hoping to head off a tornado somewhere in cottage country.

Once we were out on the highway we could tell this was no F-0. The wind was up just north of the city, at least fifty miles from where we expected the tornado to appear. Something told me this was going to be the best day of my storm-hunting career. They were talking about it on the local music station. A tornado watch had been issued. One had already touched down in Arthur, about thirty miles to the southwest. Three tornadoes were cutting parallel paths through the centre of the province in the direction of Lake

Simcoe, they said. Little Falls lay in the path of the largest. Every ten minutes we radioed into the centre for an update. I studied the clouds racing along the horizon, black and purple, as my father got the latest on the storms. Sightings were flooding in.

"She'd do better to dissipate right now," he said. "That's all I can say." He shook his head. "Even Will Keller wouldn't be able to get out of this one alive."

Anyone involved in storm watching knows the story of Will Keller, how he was sucked up into the eye of a tornado one day in 1928 while out walking his dog in Dodge City, Kansas, and spat back out again a mile away, bumped and bruised, and how he lived to tell about it. That was the only recorded case of someone coming out alive from the centre of a full-blown tornado, which is what we had here. Of course I knew the story from my father. I knew the odds of surviving something like that were astronomical, something like one in a million. I knew we couldn't reasonably hope against odds like those. They'd already reported wind speeds of 130 km/h, enough to lift the roof off a house.

The police had blocked all major arteries into Little Falls by the time we got there. The sun had disappeared. All traffic was going the other way. I recognized some other storm watchers by the cars they were driving, including the old lady who'd fed me chocolate cake after that first baby tornado outside of Delhi years before. Everyone was turning back except my father. A policeman dressed in an orange and yellow rain suit stood at the side of the road directing traffic. My father picked at the steering wheel with his thumbnails and looked over to me, as if to ask what I thought we should do. He slowed the car. Then a mischievous smile came over his face. He locked his elbows against the wheel and drove past the barricade. The policeman yelled something to us and blew into his whistle and waved his arms. But we drove right through. My father's face was lit up now. He quickly turned down the first side road we came to.

He pulled over on Ravina Crescent and we waited there, the windows up, the car rocking slightly in the wind, a few hundred feet north of where we hoped the tornado would pass. We couldn't be sure we weren't in its path. The pad my father took notes in remained unopened on the dashboard, beside the CB. I could tell he was too excited to record his observations as he usually did. He rubbed one hand over his thigh. I looked up and down the street for any indications of storm movement. Out of the corner of my eye I saw my father's face working, the look I'd seen him get before, the look a boy gets when he's figuring out how to do something he's not supposed to. I knew he was considering jumping out of the car, but I was ready to grab him if he tried. He'd already undone his seat belt; his hand rested on the door handle. He was thinking about Will Keller.

I spun the radio dial until a local station came clear through the static. A calm female voice was reading through proper tornado procedure. *Find shelter,* she said. *Preferably a basement. Stay out of cars. Close all windows. If you don't have a basement, lie beneath heavy furn—* and then at 4:52 the radio went silent. The tornado came up out of the southwest with the sound of an approaching freight train, cutting a three-hundred-foot swath through the town. One of the first things it took down was the power station. Moments later we watched as the roof of the Dominion Super Market three blocks away was racked from its moorings and lifted into the dark funnel. I gripped my hands together tightly. The car shook, the air shuffled with debris, and I felt a strange sucking pressure on my lungs. I tried to remember what my father had always said to me, his refrain in Latin—*In scientia est salus.* In my mind I ran through everything I knew about tornadoes. I recalled the great men and events in weather history: Aristotle's treatise on weather science in 350 B.C.;

Galileo's invention of the thermometer; the commencement in 1664 in Paris of the first formal weather observations. I imagined the reaction of Professor Fujita on learning of this storm the following morning. I watched a large plate of sheet metal rise in the sky over a block of houses and dive suddenly, cutting deep into the hood of a parked car. The sound of a freight train grew louder. The names and dates of famous tornadoes and hurricanes flashed before my eyes: Camille, 250 dead; Agnes, 130. I saw the route of the 1925 Tri-State tornado that killed 689 people.

Suddenly a gust of wind whipped against my face. The door flung open. "Don't," I yelled, turning, but I was too late. My father was already out there. He stood in front of the car, leaning into the storm. Projectiles flew through the air. A gust of wind came up against the car and slammed the door shut. The air around me fell still. From inside the car the tornado seemed to move at half speed, as if the storm were some deliberate act of vengeance, calculating and severe, like a torturer exacting a precise, exquisite pain from the body of his victim. Diane, 200.

I felt the nose of the car dip. My father clambering up onto the hood. I could have touched his leg if it weren't for the windshield. I watched as he got his balance. His open jacket flapped madly in the wind. He leaned forward into the storm and, in a gesture of welcome, opened his arms and shook his head in wonder. Against the winds his body snapped forward and back in quick, rhythmic waves, like a dancer's. The winds continued buffeting the car. He held his arms out from his sides and formed a cross with his body and then, slowly closing his arms around himself, he embraced the storm. His head rolled loosely on his neck and a gust of wind jerked back his hips. I blinked and felt the hood of the car jump up. When I opened my eyes again he was gone. He'd disappeared. Will Keller, I thought. I looked at the funnel spinning past us and for a moment I imagined him in there, cut to pieces by the tons of debris it was carrying. But I knew that wasn't possible. The tornado hadn't come close enough. I'd be in there, too. I opened the door and ran around to the front of the car.

"Peter," he yelled. The roar of the freight train speeded by. He was lying on the ground, face up, smiling. "Decided to come out for some fresh air?"

He wasn't hurt. He'd only been knocked over by the wind. He was laughing to himself. But he also seemed embarrassed. "Wasn't that something!" he kept saying. "Wasn't that something!"

The tornado went northeast from there. He talked a mile a minute all the way home. "Did you see that? An F-5. Can you believe it! That was a real F-5." Fire trucks and ambulances raced past us in the other direction. The roads were strewn with debris. "The whole country's going to hear about this one," he said. "You can be sure F-5s make it to national news." At Cookstown we turned onto 89 and then headed south on 27. "You can be sure she sucked up a cow or two. Literally swept me off my feet," and he laughed again and rubbed his thigh with his right hand.

We saw the broken window almost two hours later when we pulled into the driveway. Glass was scattered over our front porch. Broken from inside the house. I walked through the door ahead of my father and almost tripped over the coatrack in the foyer. The love seat had been thrown to the middle of the living room, its stuffing billowing through cuts in the fabric like a cluster of cumulonimbus clouds. My father sat down at his desk, a cupped hand over his mouth. Silently I walked through the house. Glasses and plates and Tupperware containers littered the kitchen floor. The letter my mother had left behind was lying on the floor in the sunroom beside an overturned vase of dried cattails. I didn't open it. I went back to the living room and placed the sealed envelope in front of my father. He looked blankly through the front window. I walked out to the swimming pool, took my shoes and socks off, and hung my feet over the edge into the water. I watched the afternoon light shift, shadows disappearing from the lawn, and wondered at this passion for wind, so long in Ruby's veins, carried up through three generations, how it had scattered us so far away from ourselves.

Back in Chicago, a month after my return, I discovered Will Keller's name in the writings of the Austrian weather theorist and theologian, Konrad Solovine. That afternoon I looked out my attic window and watched a grey wind carry a swirl of autumn leaves north along Palmerston, then scuttle them on the spokes of a bike chained to a young oak across the street. I turned back to the Solovine book, opened to a short chapter called "Vortex Inertia." It was a new theory he was trumpeting: the state achieved, he argued, when colliding winds and chaotic motion are replaced by a perfect harmony of wind speed and direction, air pressure and temperature, effectively creating a calm in the eye of a tornado. As a result of this inertia, somebody held in the eye of a tornado might believe himself to be at perfect rest, for his position will be static relative to the objects immediately present. When this inertia breaks down, however, an individual caught in the tornado will either be cut to pieces or ejected from the vortex. It is plausible, concludes Solovine, that Will Keller might not have fully understood that his life was in danger until he was cast out of the storm, and that the countless people who have lost their lives in tornadoes over the broad sweep of time enjoyed, for at least a fleeting moment before the end came, the sensation of relative calm.

VI

━━━◉━━━

Before the age of thirty she was already a master of the killer's art. Two-time world champion fencer and not once had she drawn the blood of an opponent. This, the sisters thought, was the aesthetics and mastery of death. They'd heard when she moved it seemed as if nothing could touch her. The strategies for killing seemed as theoretical as chess. Helen Mayer was the only Jew there that year to serve on the German team, and this at the insistence of the Americans, who'd threatened to boycott. The two sisters spoke of the fencer with a mix of admiration and disgust. They were both seamstresses, stitching their way out of the Berlin ghetto. They spoke of the fencer as they made their way back from the market, shopping carts in tow behind them. Greta waved to a neighbour sitting in his doorway, out to smell the rain-freshened afternoon, this July turn of day. He told them that the fencer had saluted Hitler from the podium that after-noon, then quickly left for America.

SPAIN

ONE SATURDAY, in the middle of summer, Suzanne came into the bar finally, almost an hour late, and told me her Spanish love story. It happened in a small town where she lived for two years when she was in her mid-twenties and I was still in Chicago. At the time I had my own ideas about what it would be like to live over there, in Spain, or somewhere else in Europe, like where my parents had come from. I remember glancing up to the TV in the far corner of the bar while she talked. It was balanced on a small shelf above some empty beer cases, the sound down, tuned to two fencers crossing swords in Seoul. I watched the thrust and jab, thrust and parry ten thousand miles away, moving my eyes between Suzanne's and the TV.

Anna used to have her special kids on Saturdays. Summer school for the gifted. That's when I'd take the Bathurst streetcar down to meet Suzanne at the Greeks, a café in Kensington Market peopled by those who seemed closer in spirit to what I was living then, in 1988, two years back from university, that desperate feeling of a place you recognize but no longer understand. In the six years I'd been away I'd learned Spanish. After graduating, I couldn't find anything in meteorology; but the second language had helped land a job working with a new generation of war babies that was arriving to this country. I started working with people who reminded me of my parents, grateful and often bitter and always heavy with nostalgia. Now they came from Santo Domingo, Guatemala City, the high reaches of the Andes. They came from different places than the places my parents and their people had been forced to leave mid-century. But they came just the same, men and women and children, all wandering the globe, always with thoughts of the people they'd left behind.

Suzanne and I would meet at the Greeks before going upstairs to her friend's apartment. She was usually late. So I'd wait there alone, watching the regulars still as statues, sipping beer. I watched the men who reminded me of my uncle from Germany, the fish eyes, shifting hands. The men who'd waited silently in the day-to-day rush of family, patiently waited for the right moment to reveal the dark secret that left them here, brotherless among their kind. I believed they all had their secrets. I rolled my own over my tongue as I watched and waited, picturing grim stories of war and deceit and ruin.

In the Spain story, Suzanne lived in an ancient three-storey building, dead centre in the middle of the old city—picture perfect, she said that day after she finally came. Everything was very old. Not like here. On her street there was a building so time-worn that it could no longer stand under its own weight and had to be supported with fat wooden beams. She remembered getting off the train, she said, grimy and tired after sixteen hours from Paris, feeling her heart drop when she saw the town for the first time. She found her way from the station and took a room in a *pension* close to where she ended up living that first year. That night she found a seat at a brightly lit coffee bar and watched the crowds go by until two in the morning.

"It makes me cringe to think how stupid I was," she said with an exaggerated look in her eyes. "I didn't speak a word of Spanish." Over her right shoulder men in white face masks touched swords.

The first thing she did when she moved into the apartment was her laundry. After she finished hanging it out to dry in the sun on the iron railing of the balcony, a man with great circles under his eyes and nicotine stains dripping from his moustache came to her door and started yelling at her. When he realized Suzanne didn't understand him, he pointed to the clothes on the iron railing and waved his finger in the air, making a clicking sound with his tongue. *Tut, tut, tut.*

"I found out later they don't let you hang out your laundry in the older parts of the cities," she said. "It's bad for tourism because it wrecks the scenery."

She told me about the writing on the walls of the buildings in the old city there, places like the university or either of the two cathedrals, sometimes even on private houses. They used to write names on the porous sandstone with a mixture of bulls' blood and olive oil. "If you were important enough, that is." Today you can still read the names of famous scholars and politicians soaked into the side of a lecture hall or library, although the colour may be a bit faded by now. She sipped from her beer. I imagined the slash of metal ringing between the swords. "Big red flowing letters," she said. "The size of your arm."

I worked at the Centre for Spanish-Speaking Adults on College Street then, above a hardware store in the middle of

Little Italy. My job was to familiarize new immigrants with the mysteries of Canada and help families settle into a new life. A job that didn't really exist when my parents came over. I spent my days talking to immigration lawyers, landlords, clerks in the OHIP office, potential employers. Sitting at my desk, talking on the telephone or interviewing new arrivals, I could hear the sound of five English classes in progress through the light cork walls of my office.

Anna worked up in Forest Hill at a small alternative school that catered to liberal-thinking parents with lots of money. She used to teach all subjects, though she was really only qualified in the visual arts. She'd been working at the Adrian Parks School for barely four months. By the time Suzanne told me her Spain story, Anna was already fed up. She hated her regular kids, she said. They were all spoiled rotten. She was thinking about looking for another job. But the special kids that summer were something different.

That summer there were always lots of work-related things to do after we shut down the centre for the night. There were Latin dancers and fund-raisers, some sort of function at least once a week. Though she didn't speak any Spanish, Anna would usually come along. She said she liked the parties because they were interesting. She said she liked to hear me speak Spanish. "Exotic" was the word she used when she talked with her friends.

We spent our evenings at home between fund-raisers thinking about what sort of future we saw for ourselves. We were always talking about the future. I'd pick up some fresh pasta after work from one of the Italian food shops near the centre. Then after getting cleaned up at home we'd walk down to Bloor if we needed anything. After supper we'd take walks through the treed backstreets of the Annex, pausing under the big maples and spruce, fooling ourselves into believing that we were in a small town in a foreign country. Spain or Mexico, maybe. Maybe one of those places that was sending all those new war babies.

Suzanne lived just a few blocks north of us, where the houses were bigger and older, like the trees. We'd taken to passing her house on our late-night walks. I knew Suzanne spent her days there—for the last year, anyway, since I'd known her—working as a freelance editor. Anna would look at all the houses along the way as we walked, shadows living and dying beneath the street lamps, briefly illuminated homes for searching blind June bugs. Anna stepped carefully as she contemplated a house we were passing, sitting there in its cocoon of dark vines. Its fine lattice-work, carved gabling, the beige, shadow-painted brick half-covered with creeping octopal ivy. She spoke of the houses along the way as if each contained a secret of its own, something to discover and hope for. I'd watch our shadows push and pull between the street lamps, not as careful about the bugs crawling on the sidewalk through circles of light, and think about my Saturdays with Suzanne. When we passed her house I'd look up and see the glow from her attic window out of the corner of my eye. Careful not to turn my head. Careful not to throw myself off balance. Just the blur was enough to send my imagination running, to imagine her sitting at her desk, twirling her hair like she did. I'd remember something about her, the way she smelled the first night at one of those Latin dances where we first met. The dab of vanilla she wore on her shoulders.

The danger of being so close to her house with Anna next to me holding my hand would send a sensation up through the back of my neck, something tingling and unknown. I'd think about Suzanne suddenly appearing in front of us on her way home from a bar or a movie. I'd wonder if she'd know enough to walk by. Would she be a stranger to me? By then she knew Anna and I were living together. Or would she want to challenge my loyalty, to see how far I would bend for her?

I used to try not to call during the week. I'd learned my lesson about trying to arrange for something sooner. I'd tried more than once. She'd told me only Saturdays were possible—and then only sometimes. Some days, like the day she told me the Spain story, I'd wait at the café below her friend's apartment for an hour and more and watch the dried-fruit vendor across the street through the front window and think about how the war must have changed my mother. She'd told me about that train ride east that she and her mother and her brother Günter had endured for weeks after the end of the war. She remembered riding a cattle car east through unknown country over great tracts of flat, snow-blown plains, along the shores of frozen iron-grey lakes, until finally the train stopped at a small road that cut over the tracks at the edge of the sea that they suspected was the Baltic Sea. They had little food. She said sometimes years later out of nowhere the smell of the open toilets steaming in the far corner of the wagon would come back to her and she'd have to wash her hands to make it go away. When the boxcar finally stopped, two drunk soldiers pulled open the door and started searching for the least starved among them. They found my grandmother and pulled her away from her children and they proceeded in the middle of the floor, her neck and legs exposed to the frozen air. The other men and women in the freight car, many of them from the same town, cast down their eyes. My mother's brother looked out the open door at the snow falling over the frozen sea. My mother raised her hand and covered his eyes. Then an officer stepped up into the wagon and grabbed a fistful of the first man's hair and unholstered his side arm. He pulled back the head and fired once into the temple. An old woman stepped out from among the silenced after the last of the soldiers left the train. She rolled the dead man onto the floor and covered my grandmother with her coat. When the train started to move again, two men came forward and rolled the body from the boxcar into the snow.

That was the type of story my mother told. Now, another type of story, this one youthful and romantic. I watched Suzanne's face, then looked up and saw the Olympics playing out on the TV in the far corner of the bar. I wondered how much I'd changed since Ruby had died. I didn't know anymore. I'd lost track of myself. But I knew, at twenty-nine, I'd become someone she wouldn't have recognized. As my mother, in her way, had been changed by the war so many years before.

By the time Suzanne found her apartment in Spain and had settled in, she'd met the two old sisters who ran the corner store three doors down from her where she bought her wine and bread every day. At first the women were suspicious of her, such a young woman travelling alone. It was asking for trouble. But within a week Suzanne's hunger for the language that came to them so easily won the women over.

Before her Spanish classes began in early October, when the old women were the only people she knew, Suzanne would go for long walks around the neighbourhood to fill her days. She spent her first three weeks feeling homesick and wondering why she'd come to such a small backwater town. She considered leaving for Madrid or Barcelona or Bilbao where she thought she'd be able to find more people like herself.

Across from the sisters' shop there was a small bar that catered to the university students in the area. This is where they came to blow off some steam after class. They sat around small wooden tables shelling sunflower seeds in one swift motion with their front teeth and right hand, drinking cold beer from brown litre bottles with the other. She went into the bar the day she moved into her apartment. It was dark and full of smoke, although the sky was clear and the door to the street was open. She managed to order what everyone else was having. But when she tried to eat her sunflower seeds as gracefully as they did, she ended up feeling awkward and left before finishing her beer and never returned.

In the evening people from this bar spilled out onto the narrow street with their litres of beer and finished the night by breaking the bottles on the road. The sound of shattering glass frightened her that first night alone in her apartment. She thought the bottles were meant for her. She thought that she'd offended someone at the bar. But after she saw broken glass on the road in other neighbourhoods she realized this was nothing but a student ritual to be suffered by the whole town. It wasn't long before she learned to tread over the broken glass in her doorway like an experienced and indifferent firewalker.

The first day of class, a tall good-looking man in his early twenties sat next to Suzanne. Reeves, from Louisiana, he said. He'd been studying art history at NYU before he decided to come to Spain. He told her he wanted to learn the language because he was planning to do graduate work in Madrid. At first Suzanne wasn't interested, she said. She didn't like his accent. She thought he was obvious.

After that first class some people from the group stayed and talked about their reasons for coming. Their foreigners' voices echoed through the empty marble hallways. There was a man from Southport, England, named Simon. He wasn't yet out of his teens. "My father made me come here," he said with a grin on his face. "He practically put me on the plane and told me not to come home till I could count from zero to a hundred backwards in Spic. Bloody jolly, he is. Christ!"

The others who stayed behind—two French women in their early twenties, a German, and a Belgian, all speaking English—said they needed Spanish for their work. The two French girls were secretaries, the other two were studying international law.

"And what brings you all the way from Toronto?" Reeves said.

"That's easy," Suzanne said, brightening. "I'm not leaving Spain till I've read *Don Quixote* in the original, front to back."

That afternoon they all went to a bar called La Rayuela (one of the first words Suzanne learned, which means *Hopscotch*) and drank beer from one-litre bottles and talked about what they'd done so far in Spain. Reeves had been there the longest. He had lots of advice. "You've got to go down into the basement of the market," he told them. "It's wild. You can find anything you want down there. They even sell bulls' balls. At home we call 'em prairie oysters."

The next day the class met under the clock in the town square. Their professor, a man named Severo Ortega, said they'd be going on a walking tour of the city. He planned to show them its practical side—where to get cheap food, some good bars (when he showed them La Rayuela, Reeves elbowed Suzanne and winked, proud that he already knew the bar), the post office, the telephone centre where you could make long-distance calls for a bit cheaper than the normal phone booths. He also showed them the historical side of the town. "The true Spain," Suzanne wrote in a letter to a friend. This is when he told them about the names on the walls written in bulls' blood. Suzanne took a roll of photographs that day, in some of which she appears standing beneath the names of great figures in Spanish history with her arms draped around her classmates, smiling.

We met in Kensington because it would have been too dangerous to meet in our neighbourhood. Tempting fate, Suzanne agreed. But not because she had anything to lose, she said once. She was only thinking of the scene she'd have to endure if Anna found out. They'd met once at one of those fund-raisers. She said she'd just as soon avoid her altogether.

That summer I'd usually leave the apartment a bit after

Anna took off for summer school. I'd hang around, waiting for her to leave. Then I'd get ready. I'd shower and have a bit to eat. Everything I did after she left for work was geared towards those afternoons with Suzanne. I'd check myself in the mirror, maybe slap some blood back into my face after a late night out. Then lock the door and head down to the market. Sometimes I'd run into someone from the centre walking west on Bloor, a family I'd been working with in those days or someone who'd since moved on. Usually I remembered names and countries, what someone's particular problem was, professional training, if any. I'd speak with them in my clear unaccented university Spanish. Someone might ask me out for a coffee and I'd always decline, citing a previous engagement, something I couldn't get out of. I'd say I'd call them—we kept numbers on file—and usually did. On the streetcar I'd look around at the faces and imagine their stories in the same way Anna wondered about the dark silent houses in our neighbourhood. Where the tracks merged beneath the wheels the streetcar would shift and clatter and I'd wonder if this was what my mother remembered from her trip east up to the Baltic Sea after the war.

We'd met at the fund-raiser for a Nicaragua relief package we were sending down later that month. Suzanne was there with a friend, a woman from Bolivia—the friend whose apartment we used in those days—named Ingrid. I asked Suzanne if she wanted to go for a drink later that week. But sitting across from Anna the next morning I decided this wasn't the direction I wanted to take my life. I'd go to where we planned to meet but leave quickly if things got out of control. We'd have a drink, exchange stories. I wanted to hear more about Spain, where she'd told me she'd lived for two years.

After a few beers we'd go upstairs to Ingrid's apartment. I never asked where Ingrid was or how we'd come to commandeer her place for our afternoon meetings. I really wasn't interested where Ingrid was or our claim over her apartment. As long as she didn't suddenly come running through the door. But the possibility of problems arising out of the connection with Ingrid had crossed my mind more than once, being as closely related to the Latin community as I was. Ingrid would have friends, I thought. Things might get back to me at the office, where everyone knew Anna.

The apartment was always messy, dishes in the sink, beer bottles on the kitchen table. Dirty laundry strewn over the couch. On the wall there was a poster of Che Guevara with a circle and a line drawn through his face in red spray paint. I thought Ingrid's family must have been part of the wave of Banzer supporters that came from Bolivia in the early eighties after the fall of the right-wing government there. Ingrid's cat used to jump on us in the middle of things, suddenly moved to call attention to his empty dish or his overflowing litter box. His name was Gato, in order to keep things simple, she said.

There was usually beer in Ingrid's fridge. We'd leave a twenty-dollar bill on the kitchen table with a little note if we remembered. Something like, *Thanks for the cold ones. See you next week.* But I could never be sure there would be a next week. The idea would flash across my mind as I held the pen. I'd tell myself that I'd bring flowers next time, something more than I was.

"I guess it was around November we started seeing each other," Suzanne said, slipping out of her bra. The cat jumped up onto the chair in the corner and spun a lazy circle, pawing, and sat down.

After Spanish class they'd go off together under the darkening autumn sky to the old cafés they used to frequent. Newspaper cones on the street corners filled with roasted chestnuts, warming their hands over the burning coals. Later, around midnight, they'd make the rounds to the dance clubs. They slept in at Suzanne's until one, just before the market closed. Then back to her apartment after picking up groceries. They'd fix a big lunch and afterwards smoke cigarettes until it was time for class.

They tried to work themselves into the fabric there, Suzanne said. When they went out with the Spanish students they'd met, they tried not to speak English together, even at the beginning when they could barely order their own drinks.

To everyone who knew them it was obvious that Reeves and Suzanne had something from the start. It wasn't as clearly written on Suzanne's face as it was on Reeves's. He positively mooned. "He's almost pathetic," she wrote home to a friend. "He's almost pathetic but he's so good looking I think I can live with it." She sent along a photograph of her and Reeves standing together, still apparently only friends, beside the cathedral with the famous names behind them.

Reeves bought flowers and made Suzanne special dinners. He pampered her. It wasn't long before he started talking about bringing Suzanne back to the States. He talked about vacations up north, by which she supposed he meant Canada. She didn't think it was up to her to burst his bubble. But there was more to their relationship than romantic dinners and dreams of northern vacations. It was firm and rooted in the flesh. They were sleeping together by now (and very often at that, Suzanne added). Once Reeves brought her to the point of orgasm by touching her under the table in a crowded restaurant. This is what Suzanne liked about him, his boldness when it came to sex. During the rare nights they didn't sleep together, she made herself shiver by thinking about him. She would wake up in the middle of the night and imagine him lying on top of her and hear the exhausted breathing that always followed their orgasms, marvelling at how the smell of his skin would change just as he was about to come, and feel his curly hair brush against the side of her face.

"But he didn't have the distance I did," she said. I was on my back listening, staring up at the ceiling.

It was a cold night in February, she recalled. Reeves was carrying a wine bottle, already opened but recorked. They'd picked it up at his place on their way back to Suzanne's apartment. They stopped off to get the bottle. Suzanne said not to bother, she already had wine back at her place. But Reeves said he had something special for her. He needed to show her something.

But it wasn't wine in the bottle. It was the blood that

Reeves used to write on the cathedral wall. Where in God's name did he get so much blood from? Suzanne asked herself. This is the kind of thing Reeves did. Extreme gestures.

Come on, he said. *Watch this. I want to do something for you.*

She remembered the bone-piercing cold as he stood on the narrow ledge ten feet above her, bracing against the wind that came whistling through the open square. When he finished he climbed down and stood in front of her, breathing heavily like a man who has just committed a murder, wiping the blood on his hands into his blue jeans.

"So what did he write?" I said. I rolled over onto an elbow and faced her. That was the end of her story. "I mean, what did he think was so important that he had to share it with the whole town? Painting it like that."

I think we both heard it in my voice. I knew she knew I was jealous. I tried to stop myself but I couldn't. I knew it was the last thing in the world I should have said.

"I didn't know what he was going to do until the last minute. Until he took out the paintbrush," she said, stifling a laugh. I saw the freshness of the image come back to her, the playfulness. "But you don't have to tell me it was a stupid thing to do," she said.

"I didn't say it was a stupid thing to do."

She rolled out from her side of the bed and started getting her clothes together. I waited for a minute, watching her, wondering what to do. Then I said, "Sounds like Romeo's got a career ahead designing greeting cards."

Her tone changed after that. It was the I-couldn't-care-less tone. She wasn't even going to be bothered.

"Fine," she said. She shrugged and smiled. "You want to know what he wrote?" She was standing naked in the middle of the room now. Her bra and underpants hanging from her right hand. "He poured that blood onto his paintbrush and drew me a heart with an arrow through it. It's probably still there. Blood red."

The stars were out that night by the time I got my things together and left the apartment. I walked up Augusta, past leaning boxes of rotten fruit and vegetables stacked three high against telephone poles and lamp-posts. Small bats fluttered and dipped hungrily, snatching fruit flies and mosquitoes as they emerged from the warm garbage. People drinking in the dark up on second-floor verandas hushed their conversation when I passed below.

As I walked that night I thought about the morning I'd

spent with Anna. It was the only time of day I'd feel hopeful, when I'd wake up glad that I wasn't alone. Glad to be with someone I could share the day's experience with. But by the time I'd come home from work I'd think people wanted too much from me. That's what had led me to Suzanne, I thought, a pure selfishness that I'd hoped would remind me of a time less complicated than this. I remembered the week's vacation we'd shared in Mexico four years before, the year after we met in Chicago. How it seemed impossible that I was the same person who'd led Anna around Veracruz because she was lost without me, because I was learning the language and she wasn't. I'd taken care of her, getting things bought, food, tickets, clothes, joking with the old ladies at the market and in the shops where Anna wanted to find tourist collectibles. It didn't bother me then that Anna depended on me. I hadn't thought of it in that way.

Then I wondered where Suzanne was. If she'd left Ingrid's by now. If she was coming up through that cloud of fruit flies behind me. Maybe she'd have something to say. Maybe she'd say she'd lost her temper, that's all. Back to where we left off. I thought I'd go by her place tonight, later, after my walk through the neighbourhood with Anna. Her light would be on, glowing in the dark, inviting me upstairs.

———

But suddenly I felt the urge to go to the centre. I wanted to sit at a desk and be taught a lesson on the mysteries of life in a new country. I turned west on College and quickened my pace. I needed to turn the tables for once. I wanted to be the one to listen, to have things spelled out for me, for someone to give me the answers. The perils and the pitfalls.

It's something you get used to, I used to tell people every day. The Nicaraguans, the Salvadorans, the Chileans. The war babies. People running from dictators, ruined economies, death squads.

Relax. Feel the place out. We'll help you find work. Discover the secrets of the city and when there are no surprises left, you know you've made it your home.

I let myself into the centre with the key I always carried in case I forgot something at the office and had to return late at night after the janitors had locked up and gone home. It was quiet and dark, only the red emergency light over the doors was on. The route of escape. Like that it was a different world from the one I was used to. The day's usual commotion, the sound of crying babies and ringing telephones, the smell of coffee and perspiration. Now there was only the thin sound of people walking by down below in the street.

I walked by the reception desk and past my office.

Through my open door I saw the single white rose the old lady from Guatemala City had given me the day before. She was alone in Canada, knew nobody in Toronto, spoke no English. I'd set her up with a family that took in people who had no one else to fall back on. I walked across the floor to the other end of the room, where a chalkboard hung bolted to the wall. Every night it was wiped clean by one of the building's janitors. I took a piece of white chalk from the ledge and held it a moment. I pressed the chalk to the board and began to draw. I drew the heart I'd imagined on the side of the Spanish cathedral. I ran an arrow through it, sharp-pointed. Then I stepped backwards towards the door, under the red light of the emergency exit, and I waited like that, rolling the chalk dust over the pads of my fingers, waiting for the heart to beat in the dark. For the first drop of blood to bead to the surface of the wound.

VII

———❖———

A week after she was eliminated, Lottie and a friend rode the bus to Kiel to watch the young man she'd met the first day of the diving competition race in the eight-metre class. The lake was choppy that day. The wind lifted swaths of water like strips of dark cloth and brushed them against the sky. The weather was in their favour, the man beside them said. Our boys are used to this, he said. It was their lake, after all. From the shore Lottie watched the young men working their yacht, bringing it to the ready. From this distance she could not find the man she'd met among his crew mates. Their seven figures moving swiftly along a narrow strip of deck, thin as mizzen masts, calling out to one another. They were small and frantic looking. There were six yachts racing. She watched as they approached the starting buoys. Wind filling the sails. The sails filled the sky with flags and colours from countries she'd never known. She heard voices carry over the water and the jump of the crowd around her when the boom of the starter's cannon sent the yachts out farther into the lake, moving through clouds of rising white spray. She wondered about these countries as the boats pulled away, Great Britain, Sweden, their men working the oak and canvas and wind in a way they believed would deliver them fastest to the finish. She said the names of the countries over and over to herself until the last of the sails disappeared behind the rising black wall of water.

MADRID WATERWORKS

I DON'T BELIEVE my parents were looking for miracles in the summer of 1992, when they got remarried out on the Atazar reservoir, floating above the abandoned town where Nuria and I scuba-dived for trinkets. They just wanted a simple ceremony, they said. No frills. But a miracle happened just the same that afternoon when San Judas Tadeo, Patron Saint of the Impossible, came glistening up out of the water mid-ceremony, his red-sandstone hair dripping and shining in the afternoon sun, to bear witness to a story that even he would have thought remarkable.

They told us their plans the same day we walked them down the path lined on both sides with chamomile and purple mint flowers and *jara*, the green sticky plant that grows everywhere in the Madrid sierra, and stood at the edge of El Atazar, a natural limestone and granite valley dammed up at the far end by an enormous cement retaining wall. It was burning hot that day. A rolling slow breeze came up from the south, damp and tired, and mottled the reflection of the sky on the glassy surface of the water. The old man I'd come to know since my first dive was down there, fishing off the junk raft Nuria and I sometimes borrowed and used as a diving platform. Two large pontoons, the old rotting planks lashed together with wire and twine and strips of clear and blue polyurethane plastic. I passed Nuria the bottle of water I'd brought from the car.

Overlooking the reservoir, we explained the history of the Madrid waterworks to my parents. Nuria told them about the oldest dam in the province, an earthfill irrigation dam on the Aulencia river called La Granjilla, built in 1560. Some you could hardly pick out of the landscape, they were so old and grown over, she said; and they were still building them. There were already more than a thousand dams in all of Spain, flooding over 2,800 square kilometres. Hundreds were built under Franco alone. After the war there was a deadly shortage of power and water, and the sites best suited for the construction of the reservoirs were the deep gorges and limestone valleys like the one we were standing before. But there were social as well as environmental problems that came with the building boom. People got in the way. When there was a village at the bottom of one of those valleys, its inhabitants were forced to leave. There was no alternative. They were paid for their property and given six months to clear out their belongings. Usually a new town was built nearby and given the same name as the one they'd had to abandon. What they left behind is what brought us here. That was why we dived.

"This is where Nuria taught me," I said. She passed the bottle to my father. She'd shown me how to clear my mask of water in an emergency and how to buddy up on a single tank of oxygen. She taught me how to breathe compressed air. The water levels were higher then, maybe twenty metres to the deepest point in the middle of the valley. I told them about the trout I'd seen swimming through the streets of the town down there, some as big as four or five kilos, startled by the arcs of our flashlight beams slicing through the dark. Public bathing of any sort was not allowed here, but among the small cabal of divers and souvenir hunters who left Madrid on weekends in search of water, it was a preferred site. The area was never policed. Nuria and I never removed the trinkets we found, something most divers did, smuggling them out in the trunk of a car after a dive like grave robbers carrying off relics of the dead.

"Where, exactly?" my mother asked. I pointed across the water to the deepest part of the lake, somewhere to the left of the old fisherman. "But didn't people protest? You can't flood a town just like that," she said, unfolding her arms and snapping her fingers.

"A dictator can do what he likes," Nuria said.

My father handed Nuria the bottle. Then he leaned into my mother's ear and whispered something.

"No secrets now," I said. He pulled away and smiled. Back in the direction we'd come, the steeple of the church of San Judas Tadeo pricked the sky over Cervera de Buitrago, the village up the hill that had been built to receive the inhabitants of the abandoned town. Nuria passed me the last of the water. My parents were both staring out to the middle of the lake, at the old man fishing from his raft, I thought. I knew from experience he'd have a tough time of it today; that even stocked trout didn't bite in weather as hot as this.

In the province of Madrid that summer the reservoirs were down to twenty per cent capacity, the lowest level in ten years. There was a ban on watering gardens and lawns. They were running ads on TV and radio urging people to conserve. Don't use your toilet as a garbage can, they said. Watch for dripping taps. There'd been no significant rainfall since the previous spring. Driving along the M-131 on the way to El Atazar the day before, we passed two other reservoirs, El Vellon and, later, El Embalse de Santillana, both of which I'd fished since I came to Madrid after leaving Canada. The fishing was simple here because the reservoirs were stocked and the trout usually hit anything you offered. The locals used corn niblets. Once three boys watched me fish the Manzanares with a dry fly and pull out four decent rainbows in less than five minutes. They'd never seen anyone fish with a fly before. They asked me where I came from and I gave them each a trout and they thanked me and scurried up the embankment and disappeared over the hill. But now as we passed the two reservoirs, my parents watching the hard dry landscape from the back seat, we saw only mudflats caked white in the sun and a thin vein of water running through the middle.

"I fished there last summer if you can believe it," I said to my father, applying the brakes. We'd always bait-fished together; while he was here I wanted to show him how to fish with a fly. I told him he'd get the hang of it in a few days.

Nuria wasn't much interested in the fishing, though. When it came to water, she preferred to dive. She'd written her doctoral thesis on the drowned villages of Spain. That's how we met. We were both interested in drought. That and our Olympic past. But where I studied the clouds, Nuria looked to people. These days she was compiling a history of Spanish rain-making folklore and water-management tribunals in Valencia. She told me how people from the villages used to shoot firecrackers into the low-lying cirrus in order to force a cloudburst. More so after the war, when the drought worsened all over Spain, and when there was still an excess of dynamite to fire into the sky. For her first book she dived all the towns she wrote about at least once, twenty-eight in total. Completed the year of the Munich Olympics, El Atazar was our favourite dive because the town below her waters was so well preserved; the blue-and-white street signs fastened to the sides of the sandstone buildings still clearly marking the way as we swam, Calle Mayor, then right on Divino Pastor, the dead-end street where children that last summer might have played soccer and shouted up to the sky, oblivious to what was planned for their town. We'd already been out three times this summer. We'd found some old bent cutlery, a broach, three clay plates, and a pair of dentures, but we always left things as we found them.

Over lunch that day Nuria told my parents about her family. We were at Casa Pepe, our favourite restaurant in town.

There was a hotel upstairs where we often stayed when we came to dive. After we ordered lamb with baked garlic potatoes and a pitcher of beer, I leaned back in my chair and saw a donkey through the doorway that led out to the back patio, roped to an anchor, chomping on a pile of weed clippings. The entrance was strung with beads, which moved slightly and clattered when the wind blew the scent of the donkey in from the yard. Far below the patio I caught a glimpse of water.

There were two old men at the next table. They'd smiled at us and waved when we walked in. I recognized them. Nuria knew them by name. She took the single stem of rosemary that my mother had picked for her on our way back up the path out of her hair and placed it in a glass of water in the middle of the table. The beer came and I poured out the glasses.

My mom and dad still didn't really know anything about Nuria. We'd gotten married quickly, a civil ceremony at city hall in Madrid. We'd been living together for almost a year when the doctors diagnosed her with lymphoma. After six weeks of tests and staying up all night, talking about what was on the other side, the specialist called us into his office and apologized for the mistake and tried to explain how they'd misread the symptoms. She was fine. We didn't have time to invite my parents. The moment was ours, the wedding a kind of celebration of being alive. My parents had already heard it from me in the letter I'd written them after the wedding. But they listened silently, shaking their heads in disbelief, remembering our own terrifying experience with doctors. I watched a single tear struggling to surface in the corner of my mother's right eye as Nuria spoke.

"Tell them about the Olympics," I said. I wanted to turn the conversation around. My father brightened. The food came and I started dishing out the lamb. "Tell them how your grandparents met."

"My grandfather was a sailor, too. He was on the German team for a while," Nuria said. "Not long, a couple of months. But he wasn't allowed to compete in Berlin because of Hitler. That's why he came to Spain." She stopped and made an eager gesture with her eyes when I reached across the table and dropped some lamb on her plate. "He heard about the anti-fascist protest Olympics organized in Barcelona for the same summer. Against Hitler, you probably know about it. A lot of Jews from Germany came. But they were cancelled when the war started here. That's how he met my grandmother. She was an archer on the Spanish team. He joined a republican militia. A lot of the athletes did. They got caught up in the street fighting in Barcelona at the very beginning and got swept up by the cause. Most of them were already Socialists and Communists anyway. My grandmother got pregnant right after they got married. She had the baby here. But when my grandfather was killed she took my mother to France with all the other refugees near the end the war."

"Maybe my father knew him," my father said. "I mean in Germany, before he came here." He took up his glass and stared into it thoughtfully. He put it down without drinking. "Sure they must have known each other. On the same team. Maybe even the same crew. I might even have a picture of them together."

I started scraping up the last of the potatoes. "You could look when you get back."

"Do you know what class he sailed?" asked my father. "Eight-metre maybe? Dragon?"

She shook her head.

"Sorry, just that he was on the German team for a while before he came here."

"Josef. This is a good time," my mother said. "With all this talk of family and boats." She pushed her plate aside and held up her glass. A smile spread over her face. "Your father and I have been thinking." There was a glow in her eyes I recognized. Right away I tensed up. There was something in her voice. I had no idea that my parents had been thinking about anything other than what they'd already spoken of in the letters they'd sent and phone calls they'd made before they came. I'd expected the obvious. Day trips and walking tours of Madrid and driving around the countryside, gradually making our way to Barcelona for the Games. Talking about Oakville, where they'd resettled since their break-up after the big storm. I'd hear about the tomato plants and sunflowers my mother planted that spring, the peas and corn and the cedar hedge that ringed the yard where Ruby and I had played as kids. I imagined my mother standing beside Nuria in the Crystal Palace in the Retiro Park, talking about the glass walls of marriage and asking if we were happy together. She'd offer any advice she could and tell her that you could never understand married life until you were near the end of it and that it was a beautiful and frustrating endeavour that was worth all the time and worry we all spent thinking about it. And while they walked and talked, my father and I would visit the Oceanic Institute or the observatory or my office at the university where I'd show him my work on the drought patterns of the Iberian peninsula beginning with the end of the civil war.

"We're getting married again," my father said. "It's our

thirty-second anniversary this year." My mother reached across the table and took hold of my father's hand.

I put down my glass. This need to move back in time, I thought. Where did it come from? I looked through the green-and-white beads to the donkey out in the garden, the water in the distance. I turned back to the table. My dad smiled and nodded.

"You're serious?" I said. He said he was.

"Mom?"

Now as I thought about it, it seemed they'd been acting strange since they arrived. In the airport parking lot that first day, while my father and I stacked the luggage in the trunk of the car, he leaned into my ear and asked me how to say "I love you" in Spanish. There'd been lots of hand-holding and small, quick kisses. Nuria knew they'd had their fair share of trouble. She knew that my mother had moved out a year after my sister died. But now they were together again and I was glad that she could see them as I liked to remember them. They looked like schoolkids sneaking a kiss between class as we walked down the Gran Via in Madrid or through the Prado or the narrow winding streets around the Plaza Mayor. At the time I wondered if it had something to do with Barcelona, if this trip to the

Olympic city was bringing out the best in them, or if this new ease had come only because they were alone now with no children to worry about and only their most selfish and intimate selves to look after.

"We saw the water," my father said. "It's perfect. The raft will do fine."

At the mention of the reservoir I slid back in memory and saw the iron-rich water turning his large cupped hands a deathly yellow the day his mother drowned, his head sliding into darkness. I remembered my grandfather sitting off to the side of the houseboat, surrounded by a pile of cast-off suit jackets and shoes while he waited for his wife to come back up to the surface.

I leaned back on my chair. "What do you mean, 'raft'?"

"We're going to get married on that raft we saw out there today."

"We want to be newlyweds for the Barcelona Games," my mother said. I looked across the table to Nuria for help. I wanted her to say something about the impossibility of all this; to say we were just strangers here and something like that wouldn't go over well in a town as small and suspicious as this. Instead, she raised her glass in the air and my parents lifted their little beer glasses and held them there, waiting.

They'd do it, I knew, with or without me. I couldn't stop them. The beads over the open doorway clattered. A whiff of donkey carried through the air. Maybe they'd seen something down there earlier that day that I hadn't. I raised my beer and our four glasses clinked in the centre of the table.

"To love's mysterious ways," I said.

"Amen," they said. "Amen."

The pontoon boat would need reinforcing, but the old fisherman said he could do it with little problem. I figured he'd agree, but I didn't think there was any chance that the town priest would agree to marry two Lutherans he'd never met before aboard a rickety old boat. I thought their plans would end there and we'd be able to get back in our car and head for Barcelona. But Father Duque agreed, smiling and nodding his head, as if he saw nothing strange in this request. Nuria had spent a lot of time here researching her thesis. She'd interviewed him many times about the spiritual and social impact of the flooding. She was dedicated to telling their story. Maybe he felt he owed her a favour. My parents insisted that they wanted to keep this simple; but I knew this was anything but simple, in body and in spirit.

The next day I taught my father how to fly-fish. I thought

this might give him the opportunity to talk about their plans some more. Just the two of us. But I didn't press him. We left Nuria and my mother sleeping back in our rooms and walked down the main street of the town, silent and dark in the predawn. It was under a five-minute walk to the water. Once on the path, we brushed against the tilting mint and rosemary flowers, their stalks bent heavy with dew, releasing the smell of breakfast tea into the air.

I left my shoes and socks on the shore and waded into the water up to my knees. There was a thin silver mist hanging over the surface, barely an inch thick. I showed him some casts, first telling him how you used the rod and line in a way that was different from the fishing he was used to because the fly had no weight and the heavy line was what carried the fly to the fish. I showed him a forward cast, then a side-arm cast, explaining over my shoulder that the perfect cast dropped the fly onto the surface of the water before the line so as not to spook the fish before he had a chance to take the fly. Then my father took his shoes and socks off and placed them beside mine and came into the water with me. He stood to my left, watching me work the fly over the water, pulling in the thick yellow line and lassoing it in my left hand, working the rod in a V over my right shoulder. The line looped and straightened, then followed the tip of the rod back behind our heads. It traced long arcs through the air. The dim morning sun edged over the limestone hills and slid its cool light down over the water.

I handed the rod to my father and stood behind him and placed my knees gently in the small crooks at the back of his legs. Looking over his left shoulder, I helped him find his proper grip, arm and rod-butt positions. We practised the overhead cast first until he knew where his mistakes were. The line snapped behind our heads. It looped absurdly and touched the gravel shore where we'd left our things. He almost caught the sock out of his shoe. He brought the line in with the reel and I showed him the knots that had formed in the long thin leader that joined the fly to the heavy line, which indicated that he was returning the tip of the rod back over his head too quickly. I tried to explain the V he wanted to draw in the air above his right shoulder, the pause needed behind the head to ensure the line had sufficient time to unroll of its own will and momentum, only to be brought back with the forward motion of the rod once it was fully extended and could do nothing but come back over the shoulder with even the slightest forward tilt of the rod. It was something that came with practice, I said. You've got to find and understand the rod's energy and live that energy through the tip of the rod and your wrist and arm and shoulder. My father returned the rod to me and I cast again twice out over the water. The yellow line unrolled over the surface like a lizard's tongue, throwing down the yellow image of its inverted self onto the black water, and gently dropped a number 16 bloodworm midge pupa thirty feet out. Before the fly had a chance to sink a small trout rose and I passed the rod to my father once the trout was secure on the hook and he brought him in easily, keeping the line taut and the tip of the rod between himself and the fish at a forty-five-degree angle to the water. I stood back and watched, patient now as he had been when he first introduced me to his strange world of wind and storm. I was his teacher now. My father looked over to me smiling and then back out over the water where the fish was fighting, down there somewhere where we couldn't see him. He brought him up then and put the rod under his right arm and wet his hand in the water in the way I'd shown him so as not to damage the trout's thin film of mucus in the handling, gently took the hook from his mouth and let him swim back down into the shadows to think about what had just happened.

We practised for another hour until my father had the

hang of the overhead cast. The mist over the water dispersed and the sun was up in the sky, fully over the hills that cut the reservoir off from the rest of the world, the sky now blue and the rocks and thin spiky grass and scrub bathed in the purple light that came when you stared too long into water. We put our shoes and socks back on and walked back up the path, through the pockets of mint and rosemary, and back to the village where we found my mother and Nuria on the terrace of the bar around the side of the hotel, drinking coffee and eating custard apples. The donkey was there, still roped to the anchor, his chomping now clear in the morning quiet.

"My favourite men," my mother said. I leaned the rod against the wall. When my father sat down beside my mother, she passed him a spoonful of *chirimoya*. "Try this," she said. "I've never eaten this before." He put it in his mouth and held the spoon comically in his fist like a Henry VIII caricature as he worked the flesh off the stones, his cheeks and jaw moving.

"*Sehr gut,*" he said. We ordered coffee and muffins from José, the owner, who also worked the bar, and when he went away through the curtain of green-and-white beads we told Nuria and my mother about our morning at the reservoir and the fish that had required the both of us to land.

Before lunch we took care of some more wedding preparations. By the end of the day the whole town knew what we had planned. When we walked down the street, people called out "*Vivan los novios*" through cupped hands. Some mistook Nuria and me for the happy couple and I told them that it was my mother and father who were getting married, not Nuria and I, but it was an easy mistake to make. By the end of the night everyone seemed to have the story straight and offered handshakes and wine wherever we went and slaps on the back for my father and me. A lot had to do with Nuria, whom most people already knew from her interviews here. Even the mayor, a small man with a red face and nicotine stains on his fingers, stopped us on the street and reintroduced himself to Nuria. He said he would be pleased to help in any way he could. Our good news was welcomed everywhere, it seemed, even though it belonged to strangers.

The next morning I tried to catch up on what was happening in Barcelona. We had a TV in our room. Some events had already advanced to the medal rounds, though the Games had only been going for three days. The sailing, diving and gymnastics were yet to come. We had tickets. We'd be leaving for Barcelona in two days, the morning after the wedding, three days later than originally planned. After some boxing, a news spot came on about Bosnia. The old Olympic capital had been surrounded now for more than one hundred days, the announcer said. I turned down the sound. I was thinking about all this wedding business. I wanted us to be on our way, to get back in the car and drive. I looked back at the screen and saw a line of refugees streaming northward into the hills.

The following day, news of our first setback came. There was a knock at our door. The mayor stood at the threshold. I was in front of the TV, my shaving brush in my hand, face half-covered in lather. I'd been watching women's equestrian. He told us that engineers from the Canal de Isabel II had found structural damage in the retaining wall of Puentes Viejas, the dam in the middle of the system we were on, about ten kilometres north of here. It required immediate repairs. If it should give before repairs could be completed, it would flood both the dams beneath it and drown dozens of villages along the way. There would be a chain reaction. First El Villar, then El Atazar, where we were. We were at twenty per cent that summer. But the three reservoirs together meant more than twenty-three square hectares of water. They were opening the two lower dams as a precaution. He said they were going to drain off all the water beginning tomorrow at midnight. He'd just got off the phone with the people at the Canal de Isabel II in Madrid. There was nothing he could do about it. It was a necessary safety precaution.

When I told him we could move up the wedding, he nodded, brightening. I left Nuria and the mayor talking in our room, already making new plans, and walked across the hall and told my parents that the Madrid Waterworks was rescheduling the show. My father was standing in the bathroom door in his underwear, my mother sitting in the chair at the window, her knitting in her lap, now looking at me over her glasses. We had to find Father Duque to see if he could reschedule the service. Then the old fisherman we'd planned to rent the raft from. He was making repairs, and could they be finished for tomorrow? The whole village knew about the water level crisis. Walking through town later that afternoon, people looked at us with sad eyes and offered their condolences as if this were suddenly turning into a funeral.

That evening before supper, while my parents attended the rushed wedding rehearsal on the patio of Casa Pepe (Nuria was there as their interpreter; the donkey, chomping at its pile of grass, the only idle witness), I walked down to the water with my fly rod and tried my luck for the last time before the reservoir was drained. It would eventually be filled again, when the rains finally came in December. But the trout would be transported to another body of water, Navacerrada or Navalmedio, I guessed, released to swim among the ruins of a different sunken village. The Atazar had never been drained before. I would see what I could take from her before her waters began to rush through the sloughs at the south end of the reservoir and the rooftops of her underwater town felt time restart and the breath of air move through her streets for the first time since she was flooded twenty-two years before.

I fished the number 16 bloodworm again between ten and twelve feet down, casting in an arc from a point of land that stuck out of the shore into the reservoir like an accusing finger. I knew from diving here that sunlight penetrated only that far, even on the sunniest days, and that's where I'd find trout, just above the weed cover. I tried an olive-coloured dragonfly nymph, then an olive damselfly. Nothing was hitting. The sun was starting to go behind me. I was casting out fifty, maybe sixty feet and retrieving the line between the thumb and forefinger of my left hand, pulling it in slowly with a gentle rolling motion to simulate the foraging of the mayflies and scuds I was imitating. Then suddenly my rod bent double in my hands and I lifted the tip into the air and a trout came out of the water and tail-walked big and shining over the surface and went down again, moving quickly to deep water. I watched my reel give out, screeching. I pressed with my left hand to slow the drag. When I was down to about five yards I seized up the reel and the fish came up out of the water for a second time, almost in the centre of the lake it seemed, and hung in the air, glistening red and silver, sparkling as brilliant and bright as a rainbow. He was free before he hit the water. My rod fell straight. I sat down heavily on the shore, shaking and looking at my hands and up again to where the trout had disappeared. I sat like that until the night started in from the east across the dry plain beyond the valley. I stood up and watched it move over the land. It was like a giant man bringing his thundering shadow across the earth. I turned and walked hurriedly along the path to town and found everyone waiting for me at Casa Pepe, where we'd agreed to invite Father Duque for the supper after the rehearsal.

Father Duque was teaching my parents some Spanish when I came in and joined them. They were already into a second bottle of wine. At first it seemed nobody understood anything anyone was saying. My dad was speaking a mix of

German and English and Latin. Nuria was leaning into the three of them, translating and writing down words on a napkin. There was a plate of pigs' ears and a Spanish omelette and a wooden *tabla* of cheese sitting between them. José came with another bottle. I knew Nuria was excited about the chance she'd get the day after tomorrow to look at the town, at least part of it, when the water level was dropped. She'd slip into professional mode after the wedding, take some photos, kick around the muck looking for anything she might have missed during one of her many dives here. This was an unexpected opportunity to breathe natural air while she nosed around the village, instead of sucking compressed oxygen from a tank and moling half-blind with a flashlight. But when I sat down she tilted her head and turned serious, as if to ask me what was wrong. She didn't ask me outright, and I didn't tell her that I'd felt something strange on my way back up the trail from the water. But she knew something had happened, although I didn't know exactly what myself. She poured me a glass of wine and deflected the conversation away from me for a time so I could come back into myself.

———

When we got down to the water the next evening, half the town was gathered on the shore waiting for us. A few of the women were wearing *chulapas*, the traditional tight-fitting polka-dot dress and handkerchief head wrap typical of Madrid, a red carnation placed at the top of the head. We walked down the hill on the path I'd retreated over the night before. My mother's face flushed. She'd never seen these fabrics before. I knew she'd want to slow this down a little and talk to these women about the dresses they were wearing. Small girls came with flowers and glasses of wine and sweet biscuits and *morcillas* on silver platters. I looked to the shore ahead of us where the boat was waiting with the old fisherman there like he said he would be, the captain who would take us to sea.

We shook hands with the mayor. He looked bloated and nervous in his old suit. The dark tie around his neck seemed to have held the same knot since the first day he tied it. I could already see him planning bus tours from all over Spain and the rest of Europe. These hills and this water would be billed as the elixir of love that would lead to a second honeymoon, and a second chance for this town. We shook hands all around and a small girl in a red-and-blue dress with an embroidered apron around her waist stepped forward and offered my mother and father shortbread on a silver tray. I saw my mother studying the dress. She touched the sleeve and bent her head to admire the weave, to see how things were done here. Then they each took a piece of shortbread and said thank you in Spanish and the girl smiled and curtsied and retreated back into the crowd.

Nuria unclasped the Star of David necklace she'd worn at our own wedding and fastened it around my mother's neck. She told her that her grandmother had worn this the day she married her grandfather back in 1936. Then she kissed her on both cheeks. My mother carefully placed it under her dress against her skin, then lifted Nuria's right hand in hers and held it for a moment against her heart.

A wineskin was passed forward and I took it and raised it up and felt the wine splatter against the back of my throat. Nuria had a drink and wiped her mouth with a handkerchief she took from her dress pocket. The wine was warm already in the hot air. But it felt good on my throat and helped me breathe easier.

After half an hour of more handshakes and wine we climbed onto the small raft that the old fisherman had reinforced since yesterday with extra inner tubes and boards. Now it was as big as a small barge. It didn't seem to sink deeper into the water when we stepped on board but held its own against our weight until the six of us were ready and the old fisherman untied her and pushed us off and began working the tiller at the stern, moving the barge heavily out to open water.

There was a small altar at the bow fashioned from a thick tree branch about waist high with a square flat board nailed at the top on which rested a leather-bound Bible. My father stood beside the altar, looking down into the water. We moved over the glassy surface in small jerking movements. I wondered now if he was having second thoughts. I wondered if the joke was over for him and he was thinking about his mother. I half expected him to ask the old fisherman to turn this pile of junk around and get him back to the shore right away where he would return to his normal self. But he just kept looking down into the water, then out to the middle where we were heading, one hand in his pocket, his suit jacket thrown over his right shoulder. He was smaller than he used to be. He was shrinking. Old now, I thought. Like my mother. An old couple play-acting on this rickety stage. This shrunken man, this withered bride.

The hills all around us rose higher into the sky the longer the old fisherman rowed. We'd already been out forty-five minutes and were still going. The light-headedness I'd felt from the wine I'd drunk on shore was gone now. They wanted to be in the middle of the lake, they said. They wanted to be married again out there on deep water. The old fisherman's navigation of his newly altered raft was poor. He cut a zigzag over the water, looking back and cursing at the irregular wake, stopping mid-sentence to ask forgiveness from Father Duque who stood next to him, then crossing himself from beret to belt buckle, then across his chest. As he pulled against the tiller the sky grew smaller, the hills reached higher over our heads. I thought it was an optical illusion. I thought the magic of this place was taking over and the recollection of the big rainbow that had taken my fly the evening before was making me see this differently, grander than I'd ever known any of this to be. The people who remained on shore were specks now. But I could see that some were still waving their arms in the air.

My father came back out of his reveries and turned and motioned to the old fisherman that here was fine. He stopped and wiped his face with a red-and-white handkerchief, then removed his beret and held it with both hands over his lap. My mother and father collected themselves at the bow and Father Duque stood before them, rocking slightly with the motion of the slowing raft. I took my place at my father's side. Nuria, my mother's maid of honour, stood to her right, a bouquet of roses pressed against her chest. I straightened my tie, my father's ring in my casting hand. I passed it to my left and rolled it against the hard surface of my own ring. I looked back to the shoreline where we'd started. That's when I saw we were already in trouble, when I saw the thick dark strip of wet rock running along the perimeter of the reservoir, already five or ten feet deep. The shoreline was rising against the surface. The water level was lowering. That's why the hills had seemed to be growing, the sky diminishing. I looked at Nuria. She still hadn't noticed. I wondered who'd gotten their scheduling wrong, the mayor or the Canal de Isabel II people. Off by six hours. My parents off by thirty-two years.

Father Duque was speaking. Under his voice, Nuria translated. "With a wise and mature love," she said, "you have elected to marry again, before your son and daughter-in-law and before God."

Before God and my wife and parents I watched the shoreline rise, the dark band of wet rock thickening against the hills. A few hundred metres to the south at the opposite end of the reservoir, water would be rushing down the uncontrolled floodgates at 410 cubic metres a second, throwing up sparrows in fright from their nests within the great concrete and iron works of the dam, rabbits and lizards from the dry spillway behind the enormous arch-cupola of the retaining wall. That was a lot of water, I knew. I was familiar with the *Inventario de presas españolas 1986*, the publication that listed details of all the dams in the country. Because we were only at twenty per cent to begin with, an escape rate as fast as that would drain the Atazar in about four hours.

Then it occurred to me that this wasn't a miscommunication. Maybe the timetable had been changed suddenly because Puentes Viejas was deteriorating faster than had been expected. I knew it was an old dam, one of Franco's first, built in 1940, right after the war when cement was still scarce and of poor quality. Maybe ten kilometres upstream the dam had given way and twenty-some square hectares of water were pounding down through the valley, wiping out everything in its path. I tried to shut out the words of the priest. I listened for a deep rumbling. I felt the air for vibration. There was nothing but the scent of mint carried on a light breeze and the faint taste of wine in my mouth. My hands were clammy now. I fidgeted and watched the shoreline rising above the water. I looked at Nuria, deep in the ceremony, my father's ring slick in my palm.

I loosened my tie and turned and looked behind me, behind the old fisherman standing respectfully at attention, unconsciously fiddling with the beret in his hands. I turned for no reason I knew, maybe it was only nervousness, but just in time to see the slender steeple of the first church of San Judas Tadeo stick its point out of the water like a periscope raised up into the light and air to investigate a world it hasn't seen in twenty-two years. It was right there, ten feet off the stern. I turned just as it appeared. The slate shingles of the belfry shone silver-white in the afternoon sun. Squinting, I forced a smile for the old fisherman, then looked back to Father Duque. His eyes moved between my parents and his Bible, then up to me. He paused. I thought he'd seen it too. I wondered if he'd call off the ceremony. But he just waited, looking at me, waiting for something. My father gave me a nudge with his elbow. "The ring," he said under his breath. I felt them all looking at my shaking hand as I wiped it on my sleeve and passed it to him. My father turned to my mother and slowly wiggled the band up her finger, twisting and turning the bright gold. Father Duque smiled when he finally got it over the knuckle.

"You can kiss the bride," he said in a proud conspicuous English. I turned again, hoping that the church had disappeared, hoping that what I'd seen had been nothing more than a rare angle of light performing some illusion on the surface of the water. But it was there again, bigger now and higher in the water. The belfry silent and empty. I put my hands on Nuria's shoulders and slowly turned her in the direction of the spire. The red clay shingles of the lower roof were exposed now, the building growing like a leviathan, rolling water off its back. Bricks large and glistening and slick with algae and weed as a dragon's scales. The raft tilted slightly. Everyone stopped kissing and talking and shaking hands and turned at once when Nuria jumped with surprise. The priest crossed himself. We were near the bottom of a hollow valley now, the vermilion sky narrowing above our heads. The top half of the church continued to rise until San Judas Tadeo appeared, the Patron Saint of the Impossible, the evening sun catching him on the right temple.

The rest of Cervera de Buitrago declared itself within half an hour, like a slow striptease. It was close to dark when Nuria and I left our shoes on the raft and felt for the bottom. When I touched something hard and flat I knew I'd found cobblestone. I slid off the raft and helped Nuria down. She rolled her dress up her thighs and held it against her hips as we waded. My parents took off their shoes and socks too and dipped their toes into the water. Father Duque and the fisherman stood at the stern. "Un milagro," the Father kept saying. "Esto es un *milagro.*" It seemed he thought this wedding must be blessed. And maybe he was right, I thought, wading through the town. Maybe something like this was due a family as exceptional as ours. I felt fish tails brush against my legs. The smell of a newly excavated town mixed with the mint and rosemary that rolled down from the hills, humid in the setting sun. I wondered if I'd see the big trout, splashing like a trapped bird in the darkening shallows.

There was a celebration in the town that night, for the rebirth of the sunken village as much as for the miraculous wedding. After Father Duque phoned someone at the *obispado* in Madrid, he regained himself and agreed with everyone that this was nothing but a coincidence. There were no holy rollers among us that night at Casa Pepe where we celebrated the reception. But everyone agreed that we should be made honorary citizens of the town of Cervera, and that we would be esteemed guests whenever we wanted to return. The mayor, with a result better than he could have hoped for (and it did occur to me later that he might have had something to do with lowering the water levels ahead of schedule), hurried out of the bar and returned a few minutes later with a large wooden key to the city, which he presented between sips of wine to my father and mother, his cigarette dangling from his lips, the beautiful girl whose costume my mother had admired at his side.

I got drunk that night. I did *coscorrones* up at the bar with José. He filled a small glass with tequila and soda water, then showed me how to slam it down against the bar with my hand covering the top so the mixture fizzed and popped in my mouth and my throat as I swallowed. Some of us danced a *Sevillana*; then my father went upstairs to his room and came back down with his accordion and played some of his old favourite songs. Later he danced the *Schuhplattler*, the traditional dance of Bavaria, my mother's province, slapping his hands and palms against his thighs and rump and the sides and soles of his shoes. He could still do it, though it was a young man's dance.

The tequila hit me suddenly. I walked out to the plaza and closed my eyes. A ringed moon cast a half-light over the town. I felt it through my eyelids. I leaned against a pillar and waited for the world to stop spinning. I thought I'd only need a few minutes to recover. I listened to the sounds echoing off the four walls of the empty plaza. But when I finally felt better I didn't go back. Instead I walked along the main street to the edge of town and found the gravel trail that led down to the hollow valley. In the half-light I strayed off the path twice, but I found it again and continued down until I came to the edge of the old shoreline and stopped and looked at the church spire shining in the moonlight at the bottom of the empty bowl before me. I caught my breath and started again, half-walking, half-sliding on my haunches down the incline of dolomite and rock clay and feldspar where the day before I would have swum until the bottom levelled out. I passed the stranded raft and entered the waters of the town, cool now in the night, and made for the church.

In the relief carved above the entrance Saint Judas returned life to a dying shepherd with a touch of his hand. The scene was framed with angels. The doors below him had been removed, like many things of the town that were worth anything and could be carried away, before the original flooding. I walked through the doorway and stood a moment in the dark, water up to my thighs, the only sound now a faint irregular dripping from the rafters somewhere above. There was no statuary, no pews. Even the stained-glass windows had been taken down. I remembered my first dive here, the texture of the water that our flashlight beams sliced around us, picking a large and alien fish out of the darkness, startled by our intrusions. There had been something of adventure in those dives here, always the sense that we would discover some clue to this lost place. But now I only felt cold. The same feeling that had come over me the day before as I walked back to town along the darkening trail.

I went back out into the street and cupped my hands and brought water up to my lips. It was sweet and cool on my throat. The alcohol had made me thirsty. When I took up another handful I raised my eyes to look down the street and saw lights moving over the water. I squinted in the dark. In the distance a procession moved slowly and quietly across the shallow waters, over the drained and muddy plains and up over the hill. At first I believed it was a band of looters who'd come down this night to salvage what they could, odds and ends left behind by hundreds of families. But they were too many and their shapes were too thin, too white. They seemed to shift through one another and disappear into the darkness like candle flames, then reappear a moment later where human steps could not have led them. Some carried their possessions on their backs: candlesticks and enormous clunking radios and baskets overflowing with loaves of bread and bundles of clothing and chairs and carpets and rugs rolled up into awkward sagging tubes. But still I saw no faces. I listened for voices but there were none. I came closer, my hands tucked under my arms now in the chilling night.

How can a trick of light at the bottom of a drained reservoir convince you of the reality of what you can't possibly be witnessing? I remember thinking this when I saw my sister and grandparents and my old uncle Willy walking among the crowd. A hard pain rolled in my chest and rose to the top of my throat. There they were. Ruby's face, her quick athletic body, impatient with my slow-moving grandparents and uncle. They were in the middle of the column. Ruby moving between them, running forward a ways and returning, excited and impatient in the way she always was before a trip. They helped each other out of the water up onto the mudflats. My grandparents, both younger somehow. Come from a time I knew from long before. But they did not notice me. They walked, looking ahead and up to the hills as if there was something waiting for them on the other side.

I was shivering now. The night and the water had gone deep into my bones but I stayed and watched this procession move through the darkness, still without words, hundreds of forms, faceless but for those of my sister and uncle and grandparents. I waited until the last of the stragglers had moved far into the darkness and disappeared. A mist was rolling into the valley now. I stood there waiting for my people to return with that column of refugees, my hands in my pockets, shoulders hunched against the chill that had enveloped me. But they didn't return. I don't know how long I waited, an hour or more, until the town was under a blanket of mist and I finally turned and walked slowly back the way I'd come, found the abandoned raft, then the path that led up to town.

I heard the party before I saw the lights of the town again. I was wet and covered in mud and shivering. My shoes squelched as I walked along the main street. I stopped on the sidewalk in front of Casa Pepe and tried to brush the filth from my pant legs. There was shouting and laughing spilling out onto the street, then in the crowd of voices I heard an accordion scale, my father limbering his fingers, and he started in on the song I recalled about leaving things behind, "*Muss i denn.*" I straightened up and walked in and saw my mother and father in the middle of the room. He had the old Hohner propped up on his chest, standing beside a tall thin man playing a nylon-string guitar. My mother began to dance with the small girl whose dress had intrigued and delighted her so, its intricate weave beautiful and full of mystery. I pushed through the crowd and found Nuria sitting with the old fisherman at a table by the door with the green-and-white beads. He smiled when he saw me and leaned back and folded his large hands over his belly. She looked at the state I was in and smiled. The mud and water up to my thighs, shaking.

"This creature from the Black Lagoon," she said, touching my leg. "Looks like you've had yourself an adventure." She knew where I'd been. As she rose I took her hand and put my face into her neck and inhaled. I was glad to feel her warmth, the pulse moving strongly beneath her skin. We began to dance, my mother beside us, the small fragile hands of the little girl placed softly in her palms as she guided her over the floor. I cupped Nuria's hand in mine and held her tightly around the waist. The whole room started then, arm in arm, clapping along with this farewell song, its melody at last becoming familiar. My father stamped his foot grandly when he turned into the chorus and the words came back to me after all those years.

> *Now I must leave this place*
> *And you, my sweet, must stay.*

The music of our voices floated out into the night over the procession of the dead like shadows and fleeting spirits. The party went long into the night, the singing and drinking and dancing. There was no rush to worry the evening to a close. We'd seen miracles this day. I knew this is where I belonged, here with my people among the living.

A NOTE ON THE AUTHOR

Dennis Bock lives in Toronto.
Olympia is his first work of fiction.